I pickey and br... ...my cabin, removing the red ribbon wrapped around it. *Who could have sent me roses?*

I lifted off the top of the box and pushed aside the mounds of white tissue paper.

What was inside wasn't quite what I had expected to find. There was a bouquet, but the roses were dead. The once bright red petals were black and curling. The green leaves were crisp and crumbling and the stems were dry and brittle.

The entire bouquet was wrapped with a black silk ribbon and nestled against the bouquet was a note:

GET READY FOR A NIGHT YOU'RE NEVER GOING TO FORGET.

JENNIFER SHAW

Killer Cruise

HARPER TEEN

An Imprint of HarperCollins*Publishers*

HarperTeen is an imprint
of HarperCollins Publishers.

Killer Cruise
Copyright © 2008 by John Scognamiglio
All rights reserved.
Printed in the United States of America.
No part of this book may be used or reproduced in
any manner whatsoever without written permission
except in the case of brief quotations embodied
in critical articles and reviews. For information
address HarperCollins Children's Books, a division
of HarperCollins Publishers, 10 East 53rd Street
New York, NY 10022.
www.harperteen.com
Library of Congress catalog card number:
2007942585
ISBN 978-0-06-146874-2
Typography by Andrea Vandergrift
❖
First Edition
09 10 11 12 13 OPM 10 9 8 7 6 5 4 3 2

For my two best friends, Jim Pascale and
David Korabik

Chapter 1

*C*ute guys are my weakness.

I'll be the first to admit it.

As soon as I see one, I instantly go into flirt mode.

Today was no exception.

I was lying on a blue-and-white-striped chaise lounge, wearing the most adorable red-and-white polka-dot bikini. I knew I looked good and I could see guys staring at me from behind their mirrored sunglasses. It was hard *not* to notice. Some of them even lowered their sunglasses to get a better look.

If I were at the beach, I would just gather up my things and go home. Escape the temptation—that's what my boyfriend, Finn, would have wanted me to do.

But I was on a cruise ship, and everywhere

you looked there were cute guys. There was no escape!

So how could I *not* flirt?

For me, flirting is like breathing. It's just something I do.

I've never wondered why I like to flirt. It's part of being me, I guess. I want people to like me. I want them to see *me*—Ashley Bishop—and I don't think many people do. My father, unfortunately, is one of those people. It's hard being the daughter of a workaholic. But don't get me wrong—I know my father loves me. He just works really long hours overseeing his company, BPE—Bishop Pharmaceutical Enterprises—so he can give me, my mother, and my older half sister, Charlotte, everything we could possibly want.

This cruise is the perfect example.

My sixteenth birthday is at the end of the week. Instead of just throwing a birthday party, I asked my father if I could do something different. After all, sixteen is a *major* birthday. I didn't want something gross and over-the-top like those spoiled brats usually do on that MTV show *My Super Sweet 16*. I asked Daddy if I could take a cruise to the Bahamas and invite some of my closest friends.

He said yes.

Originally my parents were going to chaperone us, but then Daddy had to fly to Europe on business and my mother had her own job crisis going on. Because of previous commitments, none of the other parents were able to take their place, but luckily Daddy was good friends with the captain of the ship, who promised to have his staff keep an eye on us.

Anyway, as soon as Daddy gave me the green light, I got on the phone with my two best friends, Simone Greer and Kristine Fisher, and told them to start packing their bags. I knew from the start that my guest list would also have to include Tabitha Varvatos. Tabitha and I aren't exactly best friends, even though we've known each other since kindergarten, but our mothers are. I guess they've always hoped we'd be as close as they are, but we're not. Tabitha and I compete with each other for everything — grades, guys, clothes, and popularity. The list goes on and on. I guess you could call us frenemies.

I hadn't wanted to invite Tabby—she *hates* it when I call her that, but the nickname *so* fits. She's exactly like a cat—sly and sneaky! But, as predicted, my mother insisted that I give sneaky Tabby a birthday cruise invite.

Of course, Charlotte was on my guest list too, and her boyfriend, Sam. They're both going to be seniors next month. I couldn't exactly celebrate my birthday without my half sister, and I was *determined* to make her have some fun. There's more to life than just studying for your SATs.

I also invited Finn O'Brien, my boyfriend. Finn is the guy that every girl at my high school wishes she could go out with. He's tall, blond, and blue-eyed, with a killer smile and two of the most adorable dimples you've ever seen. He plays tennis and rugby and volleyball and has that All-American look that you see in Abercrombie & Fitch ads. He's definitely a hottie. We've been going out since January. On the first day of class after our Christmas break, he asked if he could walk me home. I go to school in New York City on the Upper East

Side, and I live only a few blocks from there. Anyway, instead of answering, I *slowly* squeezed his bicep and then started walking down the hallway and looking over my shoulder to make sure he was following. He was. Sometimes it's not what you say but what you do.

Finn's different from the other guys I've dated. For one thing, he's going to be a senior. Because he's older than me, he thinks he knows more than I do, which is totally annoying. He also likes being in charge—well, what guy doesn't?—and whenever we go out, he makes all the plans.

At first I didn't mind. After all, the guy usually does all the planning when you first start dating. Then, once you get to know each other—once you're a *couple*—you kind of take turns.

Not Finn.

He still calls all the shots.

Lately that's been bugging me too. I mean, Finn is really fun, but things haven't been perfect between us for a while.

"You're frowning," Simone said, breaking

into my thoughts. "No frowning! We're on a cruise!"

I turned to where Simone was lying on a blue-and-white-striped chaise lounge of her own, applying coconut oil to her glistening brown skin, being careful not to get any on her tiny white bikini. It takes Simone, who's Hispanic, only one day to get a great tan. I wish I could tan the way she does, but I can't. I'm a redhead, with super-fair skin, so I have to be careful in the sun. That means sunblock, not suntan oil. The only way I'm able to get a great tan is if I go for a spray-on.

"Where did Finn disappear to?" Simone asked, capping the bottle of coconut oil.

"She's not thinking about Finn," Kristine said from the other chaise lounge, sitting up and pushing her huge sunglasses on top of her blond head. "She's been too busy staring at Smoothie Guy."

Simone propped herself up on an elbow. "Smoothie Guy?"

Kristine nodded. "That yummy piece of eye candy behind the juice bar."

I watched as Simone glanced in the direction

Kristine was pointing. Her brown eyes instantly lit up.

"Yummy is right!" She ran her tongue over the top of her cherry-coated lips. A look that I was *very* familiar with washed over her face. I like to call it her hunting look. "I think I might want a taste of that," she said bluntly.

The words slipped out of my mouth before I could stop them. "I saw him first!"

Simone and Kristine both turned to stare at me, completely shocked. I have to admit, I was a little shocked too.

"Don't you already have a boyfriend?" Simone asked.

"Do I? I haven't seen Finn since we got on board," I complained. "I think he's playing volleyball in the pool on the next deck."

Simone shrugged as she reached into her oversized shoulder bag and pulled out a hairbrush, running it through her thick, shoulder-length, chocolate-brown curls. "That's what happens when you date a jock. Been there, done that. Get used to it."

"You're not thinking of cheating on Finn?" Kristine asked. "We already went through that with Simone when she was dating Alan, that quarterback from Briarly Academy, and simultaneously started going out with that guy who played guitar at Hunter. Rico? Tico? Paco?"

"Nico," Simone said, a dreamy expression on her face. "He was an *excellent* kisser."

"I'm so not down with lying again," Kristine finished. "Count me out."

"The glare of your halo is blinding me," Simone said to Kristine. "And all I asked you to do was make *one* phone call to Alan, telling him I was spending the weekend at your place."

"Which was fine, except that when I called his cell phone to fib for you, you were on your date with Nico at the *same* movie theater as Alan! And he saw you there!"

"Oops!" Simone giggled.

"I'm not going to cheat on Finn," I told them. "And if I were going to cheat on him, I wouldn't do it when we're trapped together for a week. I'd only get caught."

"Then why are you so interested in Mr. Smoothie?" Simone asked.

"I'm not."

"Are you sure?" she shot back, raising an eyebrow at me.

Simone can read my mind. We've been best friends since kindergarten and she's always known what I'm going to do, sometimes before I do. Like the time we were shopping for dresses for the Christmas dance in the eighth grade. While Simone was in the changing room, I found a dress that had a low-cut front and a daring slit up the side. It was just like the dress I'd seen in the latest issue of *Vogue* and I *so* wanted to buy a dress that would make me look grown-up and chic. But I knew there was no way my mother would allow me to wear the dress—I shouldn't even think of buying it! But I was tempted to. *Very* tempted. When Simone came out of the dressing room with her dress for the dance, she looked at the one I'd been eyeing and said, "Buy it and leave it at my house. You can get ready there. Your mother will never know."

So we did.

And my mother never found out.

"Yes, I'm sure I'm not interested," I answered her. "I'm just thirsty. I'm going to go get a smoothie. Does anyone want one?"

"I'm fine," Kristine said, flipping onto her stomach on her chaise lounge and opening a copy of *Cosmo*.

"I'm going to take a dip in the pool," Simone said, pulling her hair back into a ponytail. "There are some cute guys in the deep end. Since Smoothie Guy is off-limits, maybe I can get a date with one of them."

It was on the tip of my tongue to tell Simone that if she was interested in Smoothie Guy, I wouldn't stand in her way. But I didn't.

Besides, if she were really interested in him, I knew she would have made a play for him already. This wasn't the first time we'd fought over a guy.

But we *weren't* fighting over him. I was Finn's girlfriend. All I was doing was getting a smoothie.

When I got up to the juice bar, Smoothie Guy gave me a dazzling smile. "What'll it be?"

I pretended to read the menu while I secretly checked him out. He was busy rinsing out a blender, so he didn't notice that my eyes were more focused on him than the drink selection.

In terms of looks, he was the complete

opposite of Finn, with tousled black curls and light gray eyes. *Dazzling smile*—but I already mentioned that. He was wearing a white tank top, which showed off his taut chest and muscular arms, and a pair of khaki shorts that exposed his well-developed calves. He looked like a swimmer—lean but strong.

"Make up your mind?" he asked, catching me off-guard.

"I'll have a strawberry smoothie," I said quickly, hoping he hadn't caught me ogling him.

I watched as he threw strawberries and ice cubes into a blender, then added some milk. As he worked, I tried to think of something to say, but my mind was a blank. Where had my powers of flirtation gone?

"One strawberry smoothie," he said, placing the frothy drink in front of me.

I handed him my card key so he could charge the smoothie to my cabin and then popped a straw into my drink, slowly taking a sip. I'd reapplied some lip gloss before walking over, so I knew my lips looked shiny and slick.

"How's it taste?" he asked. "Good?"

I took another sip. "Very good. Best smoothie

I've ever had. But I'm not surprised."

"You're not? How come?"

"I'll bet you're good at everything you do."

Success! My flirting powers were back.

"They're not hard to make. You just throw all the ingredients into a blender and press a button."

"The last time I tried that, our kitchen ceiling was splattered with vanilla milk shake."

"Don't tell me," he laughed. "You forgot to press down on the blender lid?"

I nodded. "Uh-huh. Kitchens and I don't mesh well together. I can't even boil water."

"You can't be that bad."

"Want to bet? Last Father's Day I tried to make my father *frozen* waffles and I *burned* them!"

"You probably forgot to turn down the setting on the toaster. It could happen to anyone."

"You're sweet," I said, taking another sip of my smoothie. "Have you been making these very long?"

He shrugged as he wiped down the counter with a white towel. "Two years. I work during the summers and whenever I have breaks from school."

"What's your name?" I asked.

"Logan Gallo. Yours?"

"Ashley Bishop."

"Welcome aboard."

"Thanks. So, you might know your way around a smoothie bar, but are you as much of a disaster in the kitchen as I am?"

"I'm not skilled enough to be a contestant on *Top Chef*, but I know how to use a stove."

"What's your specialty?"

"I excel at desserts. My brownies are killer."

"I *love* chocolate, but I try to control my sweet tooth. I have too many cute outfits hanging in my closet."

"Can't you just buy new ones?"

"That's such a guy answer," I laughed.

"What'd I say?"

"Shopping's not that easy," I said.

"How come?"

"You can't just walk into a store and buy something," I explained. "You have to think of what you already own and how it fits in with the

13

pieces you already have—the color and style."

"So it's more than just finding the right size."

I nodded. "It's a matter of coordinating."

"You sound like one of those celebrity stylists."

"I'll take that as a compliment," I said. "I've actually been thinking about becoming a stylist one day. I haven't told anyone yet, not even my best friends."

"Why haven't you told them?"

I shrugged. "I don't know. Maybe I'm afraid to."

"Afraid? Why would you be afraid to tell them?"

"I know this is going to sound silly, but I'm afraid if I tell them, it's not going to happen. It's almost like making a wish. You're supposed to keep it to yourself or else it won't come true."

Logan inspected me from head to toe. "You look pretty put together. If you can do it for yourself, why not for other people? I think if you want your wish to come true, it will."

I blushed. "Thanks."

"Have you ever thought of being a designer?"

"I couldn't sketch to save my life. And sewing? I took a sewing class last semester and all my fingers had Band-Aids on them."

"You mean it's not as easy as they make it look on *Project Runway*?"

"You watch *Project Runway*?" I asked in disbelief.

"My two older sisters are addicted to it," Logan confessed. "When it's on, they control the remote. I kind of got sucked into it. Those challenges are hard!"

"So, are you the bratty kid brother?" I teased, taking another sip of my smoothie.

"Hey, I have to be. It's two against one. But Ellen and Mary are pretty cool most of the time."

"That sounds nice."

"How about you? Any brothers or sisters?"

"An older half sister."

"You must both be pretty tight."

I shook my head sadly. "Actually, we're not."

"How come?"

"Charlotte's mother died in a car accident two years ago. After it happened, she came to live with us. She and her mother had lived in San Francisco, while my parents and I live in New York City. Our father would visit with Charlotte when he was on the West Coast doing business, but she and I had never met. My father never made any sort of effort for me to get to know Charlotte. It was like he had his first family and his second family and he kept the two separate."

"So now you're making up for lost time?"

"I'm trying to. I really want to get closer to Charlotte. Even though we're living together, it's like we each have our own separate lives. I think it's because we both don't know how to make up for lost time. And we're also complete opposites. Charlotte's going to be a senior next month and she's obsessed with getting into an Ivy League college. She's constantly studying and lugging around her SAT exam guide. I don't know what she's so worried about. She's super-smart. I just want her to loosen up and have a good time. At least this week!"

"Well, I'm sure if anyone can get her to have a good time, it's you."

"I'm definitely going to try."

"This your first cruise?"

"Yep."

Logan leaned across the counter toward me. "Well, let me give you a tip, then. Avoid the nightclub on the Panama Deck. The best music is in Club Paradise. That's on the Diablo Deck. The Club Paradise d.j. is great."

"You like to dance?" I asked.

"It depends who I'm with. If I'm hanging out with the guys, I'll just listen. But if I'm with a girl, I'll pull her out onto the dance floor."

"When was the last time you went dancing?" I asked. The question popped out before I could stop it!

"It's been a while, but who knows?" He gazed at me. "I might feel like dancing this week."

"If I stop by Club Paradise, I'll look for you," I said, hoping he would be there tonight.

"I'll do the same."

"Okay." I started walking away and then turned around. Again, the words popped out before I could stop them. "I'm having a birthday party on Saturday night. It's for my Sweet Sixteen. Want to come?"

He paused for a second and I almost thought he was going to blow me off. But then he gave me a smile and said, "Sure. I'd love to come." After that, a customer came up behind me and ordered a tropical smoothie. Logan and I said good-bye and he got busy chopping a pineapple.

As I walked away, I asked myself why I had invited Logan, someone I barely knew, to my party. But I couldn't explain it. Besides, what was the big deal? Over the years I'd thrown lots of parties where I invited people I barely knew. I told myself that this was no different. I'd probably make some other new friends on the cruise and invite them, too.

When I got back to the pool, I saw that Simone's and Kristine's chaise lounges were empty, and neither one was in the water. I guess I'd been talking to Logan longer than I thought. Maybe they'd gone to grab something to eat. A little weird that they left without telling me, though. I was surprised Simone hadn't come over while I was talking with Logan to order a smoothie for herself. Whenever I'm talking to a new guy, Simone "casually" joins the conversation and "subtly" interrogates him.

My stomach grumbled, letting me know it was lunchtime. I was in the mood for some cheese fries at the Burger Shack, but before looking for the girls and getting something to eat, I decided to head back to my room. I'd finished my bottle of sunblock and I needed to get another. It was a scorcher of a day and the last thing I wanted was to look like a lobster after one day of vacation.

Once I was back inside the ship, the icy coldness of the air-conditioning cooled me off. Of course, I was only wearing my tiny two-piece and flip-flops. As I walked down the hallway to my room, I couldn't help but notice how deserted it was. Everyone must have been having lunch.

As I kept walking, I heard footsteps behind me. I turned to see if it was Simone or Kristine, but no one was there. Weird. I turned back around and kept walking, sipping on my smoothie. But then, as I got closer to my room, the lights in the hallway began flickering, casting shadows on the walls.

The footsteps started up again, and they were getting closer.

And closer.

I should have turned around, but I didn't. I pulled out my card key and began walking faster.

So did the person behind me.

I knew my imagination was probably playing tricks on me and that I should just look over my shoulder, but I couldn't. All I wanted was to get inside my room.

When I finally reached my cabin I fumbled to insert my card key and sighed with relief when I heard the lock click open.

As I opened the door, I felt a shove. I fell to the floor of my room, dropping what was left of my smoothie as I heard the door slam shut behind me.

When I turned onto my back, I gasped.

Standing above me was a figure wearing a black stocking mask.

Chapter 2

My heart was pounding with fear. It was thumping so hard against my chest, I thought it was going to burst out.

I wanted to scream, but I couldn't. I opened my mouth, but no sound came out. My voice was gone.

I wanted to run, but I couldn't. My body was paralyzed and wouldn't obey the orders I was giving it: *Get up! Get up! Run for your life!*

I stared with wide eyes at the looming figure above me as questions raced through my mind.

Who was he? What was he going to do to me?

But before I could figure anything out, something happened.

Something totally and completely unexpected.

The figure above me began to laugh.

"You should have seen the look on your face!" the masked man boasted.

As soon as I heard his voice, I knew.

Finn!

I watched as he took off the black stocking mask he was wearing, revealing his white-blond hair. He stared at me with a smug smile on his face. And then he started laughing again.

My fear turned to anger instantly and I jumped to my feet and pounded on his chest with my fists.

"Are you crazy?" I screamed. "You almost scared me to death! What were you thinking?"

Finn stopped laughing and grabbed my arms. "Come on, Ash. Loosen up! I was only playing a joke."

Finn and his stupid practical jokes! Why did I keep falling for them? I should have known it was him. He was always trying to scare me.

And I hate when Finn calls me Ash. He knows that. Calling me Ash meant he wasn't taking me seriously, which only made me angrier.

So I kicked him in the leg.

"Ow!" he cried, releasing my arms.

I shoved him away from me and he fell on top of my bed.

"A joke? A *joke*?!" I screamed. "You think that was funny? It was sick!"

"The ship is having a masquerade ball later in the week," Finn explained as he rubbed his leg. "Don't you like my costume? I'm a cat burglar. When I saw you heading to your cabin, I thought I'd play a joke on you. Where's your sense of humor?"

The words came out before I could stop them. "Maybe you need to find a new girlfriend. One who appreciates your *twisted* sense of humor."

Finn stopped rubbing his leg. "What are you talking about?"

"What do you think?" I was breaking up with him. And he knew it. I'd been thinking about it for weeks, but I kept making excuses. First there was the Junior Prom. After that there was his birthday. Then the invitation to spend a weekend at his family's house in the Hamptons, followed by my birthday cruise. The timing had never been right, although deep down I knew Finn wasn't going to take my news well. Maybe that's why I had put it off.

Finn had never been dumped before.

He was a winner. Not a loser.

And he prided himself on always being the dumper, *never* the dumpee.

But not this time.

And I knew it was going to drive him crazy.

Still, there was nothing I could do about it. Finn just *wasn't* the right guy for me.

"Ashley, come on!" he groaned. "I'm sorry about the dumb prank."

I shook my head. "No, you're not. You're just saying that."

He got off my bed and walked over to me, wrapping his arms around me. He pulled me close, trying to give me a kiss, but I wouldn't let him. I tried wiggling out of his embrace, but he wouldn't let go. His lips pressed down onto mine and he gave me a gentle kiss—a kiss he hoped would say what he couldn't put into words.

It was nice. Finn is a great kisser. But it was too late.

"You can't break up with me," Finn said,

giving me another kiss, his hands moving up and down my shoulders, gently massaging them. "If you do, who's going to give you your birthday kiss? Why don't we try to work things out while we're on the cruise? If you still feel this way after your birthday party, then we'll break up."

Oh, he was so sneaky. He just didn't want everyone to know that I had dumped him. He probably just wanted to stall me until we got home so he could make it look like *he* was dumping *me*!

I shoved Finn away from me. "It's over, Finn. We're officially broken up. If you want to date someone else while we're on the cruise, go right ahead."

Finn's eyes narrowed and he stared closely at me, almost like he was trying to read my mind. "Have you met somebody?" he asked, looking desperate. "Is that what this is about?"

Logan's face popped into my head, but I quickly chased it away.

"No, this has to do with us." I walked to the door of my cabin and opened it. "I'd like you to leave. Now."

Finn stared at me in disbelief. "You really mean it."

I nodded. "Yes, I do."

"Ashley, give me another chance. *Please?*"

I shook my head. "It's over, Finn."

Finn's face twisted with anger and then he stormed out of my cabin. When he got out into the hall he turned around and stared at me with such hatred that a chill traveled down my spine. "You're going to regret this," he said.

With those words, he left, almost crashing into Charlotte, who was just walking into the cabin.

"What was that all about?" she asked, staring after Finn. "He looked beyond mad."

I sighed. "Finn and I just broke up."

Charlotte casually closed the door of our cabin and headed over to her bed. "Well, how long were you guys going out? Eight months? I think that's a new record for you."

Ouch. *Harsh.* If anyone else had said it, I would have been pissed off. But I always made exceptions for Charlotte because she'd been through a lot—losing her mother, having to move across the country, leaving all her friends behind. I knew she didn't intend to be mean. That's just how my half sister is—blunt to a fault.

Charlotte is tall, thin, and beautiful. She has gold-flecked green eyes and long jet black hair that falls in cascading waves down her back. If she wanted, she could probably model—I've told her that hundreds of times, because she takes *great* photographs—but she doesn't want to. Guys are always hitting on her, but she rarely pays any attention. She prefers staying at home with her books. I mean, I know she wants to be valedictorian and all, but come on! Sometimes I wonder if she even knows how gorgeous she is.

Charlotte does have a boyfriend, though, a guy named Sam who she met four months ago during a debate competition, when our school competed against his. He lives a couple of blocks away from us and, like Charlotte, is going to be a senior in the fall. Kristine and Simone call him Poindexter behind his back, and I have to admit, even though he's not super-geeky, the name fits. He's more like a chic geek, with his khakis, Oxford shirts, penny loafers, and sweater vests. He has brown hair that he wears closely cropped and parted on the side, along with horn-rimmed glasses. Sam's kind of quiet and he's always polite when he comes to our apartment—but there's something about him that I don't like. Sometimes, I get the sense that he's watching me. It's not like he's checking me out. It's almost like he's *studying* me, although why he'd be doing that, I don't know. And I've never caught him at it. It's just a feeling that I get whenever he's around. Of course, I've never told any of this to Charlotte. How would I explain it? You can't just tell someone you think their boyfriend is creepy. Who wants to hear their sister trashing their boyfriend? I wouldn't want to cause problems between Charlotte and me.

Charlotte and I are still getting to know each other. When she first moved in with us, I was a little nervous. I didn't know what to expect or if we would get along, but we do. Maybe that's because we've both been assigned parts in our family and we stick to them.

Charlotte is the overachiever.

I, on the other hand, am the underachiever.

Okay, okay, maybe I'm exaggerating a bit, but unlike Charlotte, I'm not the perfect student.

My grades are okay. There are classes that I excel in, like English and History, and there are others where I'm only passing, like Chemistry and Geometry.

And when it comes to my social life, well, let's just say if they gave out grades, I'd get an A++.

Even though I'm only a sophomore—soon to be a junior—everyone at Beckham Academy, the private school I attend, knows my name. I'm the girl who throws the best parties. The girl who can score tickets to sold-out concerts. The girl who always has the latest gadget before everyone else. I'm the girl who shops at the hottest boutiques, wears the latest designers, and always has front row seats at all the fashion shows.

"My stomach is doing somersaults," Charlotte said, breaking into my thoughts.

"Are you still feeling seasick?" I asked as I watched Charlotte pop a tiny white pill into her mouth.

She nodded as she poured herself a glass of water from a silver pitcher and took a sip. "A little. Everyone says that you can't feel these big ships move, but I totally can."

I felt so bad for her. We'd had to fly from New York to Miami, where our cruise ship was docked, and she hadn't felt well on the plane, either. Then, the moment our ship, the S.S. *Celebration*, had pulled out of Miami, she'd started feeling seasick. Travel was just not Charlotte's thing.

Still, when Daddy told me I could take my friends on a birthday cruise, Charlotte immediately volunteered to help me plan things. It was the first real "sisterly" thing she had offered to do for me since moving in, and I had been touched. She did tons of research on cruise ships and destinations, spending hours online. Knowing that I wanted to go somewhere tropical and sunny, she found a cruise that went to the Bahamas and we booked it. The ship has ten decks, eight swimming pools, twelve different restaurants, gyms, dance clubs, spas, movie theaters, tennis courts, a computer center, shopping, and everything else you could think of!

"Hopefully you'll get used to it," I said. "And the pills should help."

Just then there was a knock on the cabin

door and Sam stuck his head inside.

"You ready yet?" he asked Charlotte.

She ignored his question. Instead, she said, "Ashley broke up with Finn."

"Charlotte!" I hissed.

She gave me a confused look. "What? It's a secret?"

I shook my head. "No."

"Then why can't Sam know?"

"Because," I said, not elaborating and hoping that she'd realize I didn't want to talk about it in front of Sam.

"Don't be embarrassed," Sam said. "Couples break up all the time." He went over to Charlotte and gave her a hug. "Maybe the next guy you go out with will be the one."

"Ashley always thinks the guy she's going out with is *the one*," Charlotte laughed. "How many have there been since I moved in, Ashley? Ten? Twelve?"

Ouch, again. Maybe I'd gone through a few boyfriends, but how could Charlotte make fun of me this way? And in front of Sam!

I must have had a hurt expression on my face because Sam instantly came to my rescue.

"That wasn't very nice, Charlotte," he said.

"I was only teasing," she apologized.

"Not everyone is as perfect as you, Charlotte," I said, unable to resist zinging her.

Charlotte sighed. "I said I was sorry." She took Sam's hand in hers. "Let's go have lunch. Maybe some food will settle my stomach." She turned to me. "Do you want to come along?"

I wanted Charlotte to have a nice romantic lunch with Sam. Maybe he could get her to have some fun.

"I'm not really hungry." I gave Charlotte a small smile to show her that I'd forgiven her. "But maybe we could get together later on? Unless you and Sam have plans?"

"Actually, we're going to do some SAT prep work."

"Charlotte!" I wailed.

"What?"

"The whole point of this cruise is to have *fun*. Why lock yourself away and study?" I made a suggestion. "Why not bring your books by the pool?"

She wrinkled her nose. "There's going to be all that noise."

"We'll find a quiet corner," I promised. "And look!" I ran over to my suitcase and pulled out a wrapped package.

"What's this?" she asked as I handed the package to her.

"A gift."

"But why?"

"No reason. I saw it in a store and I instantly thought of you. I had to buy it."

I watched as Charlotte opened the box and pulled out a white string bikini and a short matching lace jacket.

"We can pull your hair back into a sleek ponytail," I said as the stylist in me sprang forth. "And I have the perfect necklace for you to wear. A gold choker."

Sam stared at the bikini. "You're going to look hot in that, Charlotte," he said.

I tried not to sigh. Sam was *such* a guy. Was *hot* the only adjective guys knew?

Charlotte looked from the bikini to me to Sam. "I don't know what to say."

"You don't have to say anything," I said, pushing her in the direction of the bathroom. "Just change into it." I decided to play the girlfriend guilt card. "You don't want to disappoint Sam, do you?"

Sam gave my sister a wounded-puppy-dog look and she laughed. Minutes later, she emerged from the bathroom looking stunning.

"I never would have bought this for myself," Charlotte admitted as she allowed me to fuss over her hair, "but it *works*. How did you know?"

I shrugged, unable to explain it. When I saw the bikini, I just *knew* it would be perfect for Charlotte. I can look at something and instinctively know how it's going to look on a person.

When I finished securing the choker around Charlotte's neck, she turned around and gave me a hug. "I know you're hurting," she whispered in my ear. "If you want to talk, let me know."

I appreciated the offer but the only two people I wanted to talk to right now were Simone and Kristine. They'd known me a lot longer than Charlotte and would understand *exactly* what I was going through.

Charlotte broke our hug and turned to Sam. "Ready?"

"Lead the way," he said, following after Charlotte. At the door, he stopped and looked back at me.

"How soon are you thinking about dating again?" he asked me.

"*Why?*" I asked, thinking it was a strange question.

"I've got some friends back home. I'd be happy to fix you up."

"I'm going to take some time off from guys," I said. "Besides, I can find my own dates." I'd *never* had any problems in the dating department, and I didn't think that was about to change. It was nice that Sam was trying to fix me up, but the few times I'd gone on blind dates, they'd been disasters.

Charlotte stuck her head back in. "Definitely join us by the pool later, okay? No hiding in your cabin feeling sorry for yourself."

That was *exactly* what I wanted to do.

"And I'm going to keep an eye on you during this cruise and make sure you're having a good time," Sam said, wrapping his arm around Charlotte's shoulders.

"You don't have to do that," I insisted. I *didn't* want him to do that.

"I know I don't have to, but I want to. You're my girlfriend's sister. Think of me as a big brother looking out for you."

The words were sweet, but I wasn't comfortable with them. Sam barely knew me.

"Don't worry," Sam promised. "You'll never even know when I'm around."

Chapter 3

*E*ver since I was a little girl, I've loved getting dressed up. I live for special occasions where I can wear fancy clothes and go all out with my hair and makeup. One of the fun things about this cruise is that we get to dress up every night for dinner. As soon as I read that in the cruise brochure, I knew I was going to have a good time.

When it comes to dressing up, I have a process. First, I take a bubble bath, luxuriating in a tub of scented bubbles, exfoliating my arms and legs with a loofah sponge. Then I apply scented lotion—usually the Body Shop's vanilla cinnamon, which I *love*!—all over my body, so my skin is soft and smooth.

What you wear under your clothes is just as important as what you wear for the rest of the world to see. My underwear is always silk or satin because they feel *so* nice against your skin!

Fingernails and toes are *very* important too. Before leaving for the cruise, Kristine, Simone, and I all went for manis and pedis (we invited Charlotte to come along, but she passed). Since I knew I'd be wearing sandals and open-toed shoes for most of the cruise, I wanted my toes to look good. At first I wasn't sure what color I wanted to go with—it's always so hard to decide—but then I decided on a French manicure. Kristine did the same, while Simone went with a pretty plum color.

Next comes hair and makeup.

For tonight's dinner, I decided to go with big supermodel hair and set my locks with hot rollers. After putting in the rollers, I worked on my face, adding some mascara to plump up my lashes and smoky-green eye shadow to my eyes, with just a touch of blush on my cheeks, since I'd gotten a bit of color that afternoon. I decided I didn't need any lipstick and applied just a coating of lip gloss for shine.

Now for my dress.

Before this cruise, I'd gone on a shopping spree with Kristine and Simone and added a few new things to my summer wardrobe. It was the same day we went for our manis and pedis. We hit all the stores, from Macy's, Saks, and Bloomingdale's, to H&M, Abercrombie, and the Armani Exchange on Fifth, to funky little boutiques in SoHo and Tribeca. Everything I tried on, I loved. And with Kristine and Simone oohing and aahing over every outfit I modeled for them, my pile of shopping bags just kept growing and growing. This was the same shopping trip where I picked up Charlotte's bikini. Even though she hadn't come along, I had been keeping my eyes open for anything I thought might look good on her. Besides the bikini, I also found a really cute top and a skirt, which I planned on giving Charlotte later in the week.

Tonight I decided on a sleeveless print silk dress and a pair of red high-heeled sandals with gold buckles. For jewelry, I added a pair of gold-plated hoop earrings. Then I took out the hot rollers, gave my hair a quick brush, and inspected myself in the mirror.

Perfection!

After loading my purse with essentials like my card key, I left the cabin. Charlotte had left an hour before me, looking very sophisticated in a pink strapless silk wrap dress with Juicy Couture white slingbacks and a row of rainbow-colored enamel bangle bracelets on one wrist. She'd pulled her long hair back into a loose bun, with curls dangling on the side. It had taken her less than twenty minutes to get ready. *Twenty minutes!* And yet she made it look so effortless. How *did* she do it?

Charlotte and I had spent a fun afternoon together. We'd laid together on chaise lounges by the pool, sipping on tropical fruity drinks, and I'd quizzed her on vocabulary words. I'd even tested Sam a few times. Both knew their stuff. Charlotte and Sam were going to have dinner together tonight but we had made plans to meet later.

As I walked down the hall to the elevator, I remembered how Finn had followed me to my cabin. I chased all thoughts of him out of my mind. I was *not* going to let him spoil my evening! But I knew that eventually our paths would cross. How could they not? We were going to be in the same enclosed space for the next seven days. I only hoped he didn't hold a grudge.

From the selection of twelve restaurants on board—the ship is *huge*—we decided to eat in the Santorini, named after the Greek island. I took the elevator to the Olympia Deck and went in the same direction as everyone else. I could smell all sorts of delicious dishes as we got closer, and my stomach started rumbling. I couldn't wait to eat!

When I got to the dining room, I stood at the top of a grand curving staircase, staring at the scene before me.

The dining room walls were painted a light blue, the carpet was the color of sand, and the chandeliers were lit with diamond-shaped bulbs. The tables were set up with white china, sparkling glass, and shiny silverware. Everywhere I gazed there were couples laughing and talking. Some of the older men were in tuxedos, while the women they escorted were wearing evening gowns and dazzling jewels. Younger couples were dressed a bit more casually, showing off their tans. The girls were in sundresses and the guys were wearing white pants and tropical shirts.

It all looked like something out of a movie.

And I was part of it!

I hurried down the steps, eager to find Kristine and Simone. The descent was steeper than I thought and I almost missed a step. Luckily, I managed to grab the banister in the nick of time.

I searched the dining room until I found Kristine and Simone sitting at a corner table. They gave me a wave to catch my attention and I hurried over to join them. Both had gotten as dressed up as I had. Simone was wearing a chiffon giraffe-print halter top over a white skirt, while Kristine was wearing a floral-print strapless dress. Simone had used a flat iron on her curls, so her hair was a long straight sheet tossed over one shoulder, while Kristine had decided to go with a sleek ponytail.

As soon as I sat down across from them, Simone gave me the third degree.

"It's about time you showed up. We were starting to wonder where you were."

"We're starving!" Kristine chimed in,

handing me a menu. "I think I'm going to start with the fried goat cheese."

"I was getting ready," I said, taking a peek at the menu. There were so many scrumptious dishes to choose from. How would I ever decide?

"For whom?" Simone inspected me from head to toe. "You're looking *fine* tonight. *Very* fine."

"What are you talking about?" I laughed, putting down my menu and taking a sip of water.

"Don't play little Miss Innocent," Simone said. "You didn't get yourself all glammed up just for dinner with us."

"Yes, I did!"

"Really?" Simone asked skeptically. "It had nothing to do with him?"

"Who?"

Simone pointed across the dining room at Logan, who was lifting a tray of dishes over his shoulder. He looked dashing in his black dinner jacket and tie. If he wasn't carrying that tray, he could have passed for one of the guests. I couldn't help but smile as I stared at him.

"Look at the way she's smiling at him!" Kristine exclaimed.

Simone pounced. "You're smitten. Don't deny it! Anyone looking at you can see it."

"Shh!" I warned them. People were looking at us, including a blond waitress.

"I don't know what you're talking about," I told Simone. "Why would I get dressed up for Logan?" I asked.

Or had I? I *hadn't* looked my best when he saw me at the pool earlier, all hot and sweaty, so I definitely wanted to make a better impression. But I certainly wasn't trying to get his attention.

"She got his name!" Kristine squealed. "Ooooh, tell us what happened when we left the pool. Tell! Tell!"

"I would have told you then if you hadn't both disappeared," I said. "Where were you two all day?"

"Well, I was getting pampered with a day of beauty at the Glamorama," Simone confessed. "I had a hot stone massage, a seaweed wrap, and then a facial. We should all go together later in the week!"

"There's a ballet company on board and they were performing *Swan Lake*," Kristine said. "So I went to see that. Then I went to my cabin to get ready for dinner."

"What were you up to this afternoon?" Simone asked. "Chatting with Logan? I'll bet Finn didn't like that."

Finn. I still had to tell them about our breakup. I didn't think it would be a big surprise. I'd been complaining about Finn for the last few weeks, and Simone and Kristine had both suffered through it. They hadn't given me any specific advice except to say I'd eventually know what to do.

I took a deep breath and said, "I've got some news."

"So do we!" Kristine announced.

"My news is bigger than yours."

Kristine shook her head. "I don't think so. This is major. Huge!"

Huge? What could their news possibly be? I wondered.

"You first, Ashley," Simone insisted, jarring me out of my thoughts. "Don't keep us in suspense."

"Finn and I broke up," I said. "Actually, I broke up with him."

"How'd he take it?" Simone asked matter-of-factly.

"He wasn't too happy," I admitted.

I relayed the story of what had happened in my cabin. As I expected, Simone and Kristine were both on my side.

"What an idiot!" Simone fumed. "He thought that was funny? That was stupid. Not to mention *creepy*! I always thought he was an empty-headed jock. Nice of him to finally prove it."

"But maybe it has something to do with the ship," Kristine whispered, gazing around the dining room with wide eyes. "I think it's haunted."

"Huh?" I asked, not knowing what she was getting at.

"Taylor Morton," she said. "That's our news."

"Who's Taylor Morton?" I asked, still not following her. The name rang no bells with me. Was she someone we went to school with?

"Are you serious?" Simone asked. "She was

all over the news last summer."

"I'm drawing a blank. Besides, I was on vacation in London last summer with my family, remember? We missed a lot of U.S. news."

"Taylor Morton was a sixteen-year-old girl who disappeared last summer while she was on a cruise with her family," Simone explained.

"*This* cruise," Kristine added worriedly. "She was on this very same cruise with her family and she just disappeared one night. The ship was searched from top to bottom but she was never found. No one knows what happened to her."

"They think she might have fallen overboard," Simone said.

"But what if she didn't?" Kristine asked.

"What else could have happened to her?" I shot back. I hate to admit it, but I was getting goose bumps. In five days I was going to be the exact same age as Taylor Morton, but I was still alive.

Taylor was . . . dead.

"What if she was murdered?" Kristine asked.

"*Murdered?*" I repeated.

Kristine nodded her head ominously. "Don't you think we should have been warned before we got on board? For all we know, there's a psycho on the loose!"

I couldn't help it, but I laughed. Kristine was *so* melodramatic. She was always jumping to conclusions and assuming the worst. Like when we planned a surprise party for her last year. When we got to her family's dark town house, she assumed burglars were inside because the living room light wasn't on. She kept insisting that her parents *always* kept the living room light on, even when they went out, and something had to be wrong. We had to practically drag her into the town house so everyone could jump out and yell SURPRISE when the lights were flicked on.

"This isn't funny!" Kristine snapped.

"I'm sorry, I didn't mean to laugh," I said, trying to hold back a snicker. "But come on, Kristine. Get real! There isn't a psycho on the loose."

"How do we know that?" she asked. "Taylor's killer could be waiting on board to kill again. That kind of stuff happens, you know?" She gazed around the dining room as if she was expecting a hockey-mask-wearing killer to lunge out at her with a bloody knife. "One of us could be next!"

I bit down on my tongue to keep from laughing again. I could see that Kristine was really spooked and I wanted to calm her down. I avoided eye contact with Simone, whom I knew would only try to make me laugh. That was her usual m.o. when Kristine overreacted.

"Who told you about Taylor Morton?" I asked.

"She did," Kristine said, pointing out a waitress whose blond hair was in a short, sassy bob. It was the same waitress who'd overheard Kristine and Simone say that I liked Logan. With my luck, she was probably a friend of his and would tell him. Great!

I tried to catch the waitress's eye but I didn't need to. She was on her way over with her order pad.

"Have you decided what you'd like for dinner?" she asked with a smile.

I could see she was wearing a name tag that read *Molly*. She seemed to be the same age as us, maybe a year older. Up close I could see her cheeks and nose were sprinkled with freckles and her eyes were light blue. We were about the same height and build.

I reached for my menu. "Want to order a bunch of different appetizers and then share?" I asked Simone and Kristine.

"Sounds good to me," Simone agreed.

"I'm not hungry," Kristine moaned, closing her menu. "I've lost my appetite."

I decided I was going to get to the bottom of things. Kristine was supposed to be enjoying herself on this cruise, not living in fear. I turned to Molly. "Can I ask you a question?"

"Sure. If it's about the menu, you can substitute spinach for broccoli and rice for mashed potatoes. The Greek salad is to die for and the stuffed grape leaves are really yummy."

"It's not about the menu."

"One of the buffets, then? There's one on each deck. At midnight there's the Chocolate Lovers Fantasy on the Panama Deck. If you're a chocoholic, you'll be in heaven."

"I actually had a question about Taylor Morton."

Shock washed over Molly's face. "Wh-what?"

"My friends said you told them about her."

"Yeah. So?"

There was no mistaking the tone in her voice. It said *back off*! But why be so defensive? *Molly*, after all, was the one who had spooked Kristine.

"Can you tell me what you told my friends?"

Molly shrugged and seemed to relax. "Sorry I snapped at you," she offered. "Taylor is just a sensitive subject. When I was talking to your friends before, I kind of slipped when I brought it up." She lowered her voice. "The cruise line doesn't like us talking about her. Bad press and all, if you know what I mean."

"I wouldn't want to get you in any trouble," I said.

Molly shook her head. "It's okay. I'll tell you what I told them, but it's not much. Taylor was a passenger on the ship last year. One night she just disappeared. And no one's seen her since."

"That's it?"

Molly paused, like she wasn't sure if she should say any more. "Well, there is more. See that guy over there?"

Molly pointed across the dining room. I followed her finger and blinked my eyes. No, it couldn't be. I glanced over at Simone and Kristine and I could see they were just as shocked as I was.

"Him?" I asked.

She nodded.

I had a feeling I wasn't going to like Molly's answer, but I forced myself to ask the question. "What about him?"

"That's Logan Gallo. Taylor was dating him while she was on the ship."

"She was?" I asked, not wanting to believe it.

A pit formed in the middle of my stomach, while at the same time, I wondered where the closest computer was. As soon as possible, I had to get online to find out as much about Taylor Morton as I could.

"Uh-huh," Molly answered. "It was one of those shipboard romances, although I think it meant more to Logan than it did to Taylor. He really fell hard for her. I guess he thought they were going to keep seeing each other, but Taylor didn't." Molly leaned forward and looked around to make sure she wasn't being overheard. "On the night she disappeared, Taylor and Logan had a horrible fight. The two of them were screaming at each other."

"What did they say?" Kristine asked, hanging on Molly's every word.

Molly shrugged. "I don't know. The fight took place in Logan's cabin. Their voices were raised but no one heard what they were fighting about. Then Taylor stormed out of his cabin and was never seen again. The next morning her parents told the captain that Taylor hadn't slept in her bed the night before. That's when they started searching the ship. Of course, people mentioned the fight with Logan and so the police questioned him. But he was cleared. They never considered him a suspect."

"Suspect?" I whispered. "Why would they consider him a suspect?"

"Why not?" Molly asked before flipping open her order pad and removing the pen behind her ear. "Isn't it always the boyfriend who's the killer?"

Chapter 4

*A*fter dropping her bombshell, Molly quickly did damage control. I guess it must have been the shocked expression on my face. I wondered if it was anything like the expressions on Simone's and Kristine's faces.

"Logan was never officially a suspect," she hurried to say. "They just wanted to talk to him. It's procedure, you know? They talked to everyone on the ship, not just him. And he had an alibi. After Taylor left his cabin, he went to play poker with the busboys from the Riviera Deck. The game lasted until nine in the morning and Taylor's parents had already reported her missing by then. Logan is a great guy, one of my best friends on the ship. I'm just telling you what happened last summer. I'm not a gossip. Sometimes I say things without thinking how they might sound. If I thought Logan had anything to do with Taylor's disappearance, I wouldn't be friends with him."

Molly left after we told her what we wanted for dinner and a hush fell over our table. But it didn't last very long.

"I know you don't want to hear this, but I'm going to say it," Kristine said. "Don't go out with him."

"What are you talking about?" I asked even though I knew.

"Don't think I haven't noticed the way your eyes have been following Logan around the dining room ever since you got here. You like him. You're interested in him. You want to date him. And now that you're no longer with Finn, you can."

"So?"

"So? So? So?" Kristine's voice kept rising. "How can you even say that? He could be a killer!"

I reached for a dinner roll and broke it in half. It was piping hot and steam wafted from its warm center. I added a dab of butter and watched it melt before taking a bite. *Deelish*.

"He's not a killer."

"How do you know?" Kristine demanded.

I didn't. But I found it very hard to believe that a guy I had just met could be a cold-blooded killer. It was too unreal.

"Why take a chance?" Kristine continued when I didn't answer. "Besides, we're only on this ship for a week. Once we get back home, you'll never see him again. Just steer clear of him."

I sighed. Kristine was my best friend and she was only looking out for me. I loved her for that. At the same time, she was being Miss Melodramatic. "Don't you think you're overreacting?"

"Better safe than sorry," she shot back.

"How about innocent until proven guilty?" Simone added. "For all we know, Taylor partied too hard after she left Logan, slipped, and fell overboard. End. Of. Story."

"But what if she didn't slip?" Kristine asked. "What if she was *pushed* overboard? What if Logan was the one who pushed her? And what if—"

"Enough!" I shouted, cutting Kristine off.

She'd gone too far! "We don't know what happened last summer. We weren't here. And we don't know anything about Logan, so it's unfair of you to be making these accusations." Kristine started to say something more, but I held up my hand. "We're here to celebrate my birthday and have a good time! Let's forget all about Taylor Morton, okay?"

Simone picked up her glass of iced tea and urged us to do the same. "To having a good time!" she toasted.

"To staying safe," Kristine slipped in.

"To a birthday I'll never forget!" I added as we clinked our glasses together.

After dinner I ran into Logan on my way out of the dining room. Simone and Kristine had already left, deciding to skip dessert, but I had ordered a piece of baklava, a sweet, nutty Greek pastry drizzled with honey. It was amazing. I planned to meet back up with them in an hour at Club Paradise, so we could dance and hopefully meet some cute guys.

When Logan first saw me, there was a blank look on his face. I could tell he didn't recognize me and for a second I was bummed. I guess I wasn't as unforgettable as I thought I was. But then his gray eyes lit up.

"Ashley, right?"

Hearing Logan say my name was better than the baklava.

"Good memory!" I said with a smile.

"So how was Day One?" he asked as he began clearing off a table, stacking dishes.

"Pretty good," I said.

"What did you do?"

I gave Logan a quick recap of my day and as I did, I studied his face. I could see he was listening to every word. Finn had never been that way! I could always tell when he was zoning out on me. Even though he would look right at me, his face would get this blank zombie stare and I knew he wasn't listening. I called him on it once, but he said I was imagining things.

As if thinking of my ex had conjured him up, I suddenly saw Finn standing a few feet behind Logan. Staring at us. And he didn't look happy. Well, tough! We weren't a couple anymore. If I wanted to talk with another guy, I could.

"What time do you finish work?" I asked the

question loudly, in case Finn was eavesdropping, which I knew he was. I realize it was juvenile to be playing these games, but I wanted Finn to know that it was over between us. The best way to do that was to show him I had moved on.

I wasn't using Logan to make Finn jealous. He seemed like a nice guy and I wanted to get to know him better. I also had the sense that he liked me too. I wondered if I was the first girl he'd shown any interest in since Taylor. Had he been *in love* with her? Her disappearance must have crushed him. Poor guy.

"I get off in another hour," he said.

"My girlfriends and I are going to be at Club Paradise. Why don't you join us?"

Logan nodded, giving me a smile. "I'll definitely be there."

I smiled back. "Great!"

Three hours later I was in Club Paradise, dancing with Kristine and Simone. The music was great. Justin Timberlake's "SexyBack" had just finished playing, and we headed back to the red leather booth where our Cokes were waiting.

Charlotte and Sam were also dancing.

Charlotte was definitely feeling the music, but poor Sam had no rhythm whatsoever. His arms were flapping like a chicken's and his knees kept knocking together. He was trying to imitate the moves from that old John Travolta disco movie, *Saturday Night Fever*, but it wasn't working. Not that it mattered. Sam was having a good time and that's what vacations are all about.

Charlotte looked our way with a smile. I waved and smiled back at her.

Simone noticed and asked, "Is Charlotte having a good time?"

"I haven't exactly pried her away from her study guides," I confessed, "but she's loosening up. We hung out by the pool this afternoon."

"It's a start," Kristine said.

"I know," I said. Kristine and Simone both knew that Charlotte and I weren't exactly tight and that I was trying to change that. "I just wish we were closer."

"Why? Be thankful for your space. My two younger sisters drive me crazy," Simone said.

"But you love them, right?"

"Well, yes," Simone admitted, "although don't ask me that when they've both been going through my things!"

"Well, I want Charlotte to know that I love her and I'm there for her if she ever needs me."

"Doesn't she already know that?" Kristine asked.

I shook my head. "I don't think so. She still keeps to herself. Even though she's living with us, she doesn't act like she's a part of our family. It's not that we haven't tried. We all have. My mom's taken her on shopping trips, my dad's taken her out on his boat, and we've all gone together to the movies or the theater. We always include her in our conversations, but it feels like she joins in because she has to, not because she wants to. Most of the time, she chooses to be alone with her books."

"Give her time," Kristine advised. "She's been through a lot and she's still adjusting."

"I know," I said. "I know."

While we were talking, I kept discreetly peeking at my watch. At least I thought I was being discreet.

"Why do you keep looking at your watch?" Kristine asked as she caught me checking the time. "You've been doing it all night," she added, dabbing at her forehead with a napkin. I was a little sticky myself. It was hot under those silver disco balls!

"No, I haven't," I said, sipping at my soda.

"Yes, you have," Simone chimed in as she pulled out her compact and checked her makeup. "Even I've noticed."

"Did you make a date?" Kristine asked excitedly.

"No," I answered. Technically, it wasn't a date. I'd told Logan I was going to be dancing at Club Paradise and he said he'd join me. That was it. But he'd said he'd be off work in an hour. Was he working an extra shift?

Kristine yawned. "I don't know about you two, but I'm all danced out. I'm going to go to bed."

Simone closed her compact and slipped it back into her purse, taking one last look around the dance floor. "*Very* slim pickings here tonight. Hopefully, the guys will get hotter as the week goes by. I'm ready to go to bed too."

"I'm not tired," I said, deciding I would wait a little longer to see if Logan showed. "I'm going to stay and hang out with Charlotte."

"Okay," Kristine said as she and Simone left. "See you in the morning."

Seconds after Simone and Kristine left, Charlotte came over to the booth. "Why are you sitting by yourself?" She reached for my hands. "Come dance with us. Maybe you can show Sam some new moves. His are about thirty years old."

"All he needs is a white polyester suit," I giggled.

Charlotte laughed. "Don't give him any ideas!" She tugged me out of the booth. "Come on!"

"Okay!" I exclaimed, following after her as the d.j. began playing one of my favorite Madonna songs, "Hung Up." After that he played some Beyoncé, Christina Aguilera, Fergie, and Gwen Stefani. As the music played, I kept peeking at my watch.

When another forty-five minutes went by, I threw in the towel and decided it was time to call it a night. Obviously, Logan was a no-show. If he was planning to join me, he would have been here by now.

I said good night to Charlotte and Sam and

was walking out of Club Paradise when the last person I expected to see walked by.

"Hey! What happened to you?" I asked, running up to Logan's side with a smile. He had changed out of his waiter's uniform into a pair of jeans and white T-shirt trimmed with blue at the neck and sleeves. The bright white nicely showed off the rich, dark color of his tan. "I had just about given up on you and was going to bed. Did you have to work late?"

"I had something to take care of."

"My sister and her boyfriend are here. Let me introduce you."

I brought Logan over to the booth where Charlotte and Sam were taking a break.

"Hey, guys. I wanted to introduce you to a new friend. This is Logan Gallo." I turned to Logan. "This is my sister, Charlotte, and her boyfriend, Sam."

Logan gave them a warm smile. "Hi. Looks like you're having a great time."

"We're not used to this much dancing," Charlotte laughed.

"You'll get used to it," Logan said.

"Are you vacationing with your family?" Sam asked.

"No, I work on the ship," Logan said. "This is my second summer."

"We'll leave you guys alone," I said, pulling Logan away. Hopefully, Charlotte had picked up on my hint. I looked over my shoulder and she mouthed one word: *Cute!*

I smiled back and nodded. I'd fill her in about Logan when we were alone in our cabin.

I took Logan's hand in mine. "Want to dance? The d.j. is spinning some great songs."

Logan dropped my hand like it was infected with some sort of contagious virus. "Not really. I'm too beat for dancing. I was on my way to my cabin."

I couldn't help but be a little stung by his sudden disinterest. And he was going to bed? He hadn't been on his way to meet me? Well, there had to be a reason.

"The caffeine will probably keep us up all night, but want to grab a latte?" I suggested, determined to salvage some part of the night. "There's a coffee bar on the deck above us. We could sit outside and talk. There's a full moon and lots of stars."

"Nah."

"Well, what do you want to do?" I asked, trying not to feel frustrated. It would help if he made some suggestions. After all, he knew the ship better than I did.

Logan just shrugged.

I was really confused. At the pool and earlier tonight in the dining room, I could sense that Logan kind of liked me. There's no mistaking when a guy likes you. It's just something in the way he looks at you. Talks with you. Smiles at you. He was interested. I know I wasn't making it up. But now he was acting like he wasn't.

"We could go back to my cabin and just hang out," I suggested. Hopefully, Charlotte would stay out with Sam a little while longer. At the very least, Logan and I could have a quick chat outside my cabin door and make plans for tomorrow.

"I don't think your boyfriend would like that too much," Logan said, looking annoyed.

Suddenly, all the pieces fell into place! After I left the dining room Finn must have told Logan that I was still his girlfriend. That liar! He was *so* dead the next time I saw him!

"I don't have a boyfriend," I insisted.

"Really? That's not what he says."

"He's lying. We broke up this afternoon."

"Was this before or after you started flirting with me at the smoothie stand?"

I hesitated before answering. Should I lie or tell the truth? I stared into Logan's face and decided on the truth.

"After," I admitted. "But I've been thinking about breaking up with him for weeks."

"I thought you liked me."

"I do!"

Logan shook his head. "No, you were just using me to make your boyfriend jealous."

"Ex-boyfriend," I clarified. "And I wasn't using you. I will admit that I wanted Finn to hear me making plans with you, but only because it's *over* between us and I wanted it to sink into that thick skull of his," I insisted. "I wasn't trying to make him jealous. Why would I do that when I'd already broken up with him?"

"I don't know." He shrugged. "Maybe you like playing games."

"*He's* the one playing games," I said. "He only lied to you to make trouble for me. I wasn't using you. I wouldn't do that to anyone, especially not someone I like. Please believe me."

"Look, Ashley, you're great and all, but I don't want to mess with another guy's girl."

"I'm *not* Finn's girl," I insisted.

"That's not what he seems to think. He thinks you're still his girlfriend, and if that's true, then you're off-limits. I've had my share of messed-up relationships and I don't want to go there again."

There was no mistaking the pain in Logan's voice. Taylor must have broken his heart.

"I don't care what Finn wants or thinks," I said. "I like *you*, Logan. I want to be with *you*. Not Finn."

"That's what you say now. But what about tomorrow?"

I didn't know what to say. It was true that I'd be leaving at the end of the week. Anything I started with Logan would probably have to be short-term.

"I better get going," Logan said. "Enjoy the rest of your cruise."

"Did a girl break your heart, Logan?" I blurted out. "Is that why you won't give me a second chance?"

Logan looked startled by my question.

"That's ancient history," he said.

"No, it's not. Not if you won't give me another chance." I moved closer to Logan and gazed into his eyes. "I'm not her. I'm just me. Ashley Bishop. I'd never hurt you."

Logan looked away, gazing out into the sea. "I don't think she planned on hurting me, but she did. I guess I'm not ready for another relationship. I thought I was, but then all this baggage popped up."

I knew he was referring to Finn. "There is no baggage. I'm free and clear." I touched him on the arm. "Can't we start over?"

Logan sighed and ran a hand through his curls. "I can't think about this right now. Seriously. It's been a long day and I'm exhausted. All I want to do is crash. Just give me some space. If I want to talk, I'll find you."

"And if you don't find me?"

"Then you know what that means," he said.

And with those final words he left me alone on the deck.

I felt awful when I got back to my cabin. *Awful*.

How had I created such a mess in one day? I wanted to cry, but the tears wouldn't come.

Turning on the lights, I saw that Charlotte wasn't back yet. That gave me a little time to pull myself together.

I grabbed a tissue from the dresser and blew my nose. As I did, I noticed that our beds had been turned down by the maid and each had a silver-wrapped chocolate on the pillow. I unwrapped the chocolate and popped it into my mouth, hoping it would make me feel better, but it didn't. Whoever says chocolate fixes everything is wrong.

Our cabin had a balcony with a wrought-iron railing. I decided I would go outside and get some fresh air. Maybe clearing my head would help me figure out how to make things right with Logan.

I stepped through the sliding glass doors of the cabin and out onto the balcony. The black metal railing that wrapped around all three sides had been shaped into a curving design of leaves and flowers. There was a small glass-topped table and two chairs with cushions, but I didn't sit down. I hugged the railing and leaned against it, staring out into the dark night.

Below me I could see the inky waves of the ocean and hear the smooth humming of the ship's engines. There was a slight breeze in the air and the coolness felt good against my flushed face. I leaned farther against the railing, wanting to feel more of the breeze. I placed my hands along the smooth metal top of the railing and, as I did, I became aware of something.

The railing was wobbly.

I didn't give it much thought, because it was barely noticeable, just a small shake. And my head was still preoccupied with thoughts of Logan.

But seconds later, as my weight pressed farther into the railing, the wobbling grew stronger.

Before I could do anything else, I heard a creak.

Followed by a loud tearing sound.

I don't know what made me do it—maybe

it was a survival instinct — but I instantly let go of the railing.

Seconds later, it ripped away from the sides of the balcony, plunging into the ocean below.

Chapter 5

As the railing fell away, I gasped and started to lose my balance.

It didn't help that the floor of the balcony was wet and misted with drops of sea spray, making it slippery. I tried to pull myself back from the edge, but I couldn't. It was like being on a wax floor!

I kept getting closer and closer to the edge of the balcony, only one thought going through my mind. *I had to stop moving.* If I didn't, I was going to plunge into the ocean below!

I felt the panic overtaking my body, and a scream lodged in my throat. I looked around for the closest solid object and threw my arms out, grabbing the patio chair next to me. I flung my body into it, collapsing on the cushions. A wave of relief washed over me as I realized

I was safe. Safe!

It took a few minutes to pull myself together. My heart was beating furiously for the second time in less than twenty-four hours, and I was struggling to process what had almost happened. I stared at the edge of the balcony where only a short time ago there had been a railing.

And now there wasn't.

Behind me I could hear the cabin door closing. Then came the sound of Charlotte's voice.

"Ashley?" she called out. "Where are you?"

I could hear her footsteps approaching and then she was standing by the sliding glass doors. "There you are!" she said, stepping outside, her high heels clicking against the balcony floor. "What are you doing out here? I thought you'd be asleep by now. Or with Logan."

I didn't say anything. I just pointed at where the railing used to be.

She gasped, her eyes widening. "What happened?"

I tried to get the words out, but couldn't. Then I felt my eyes filling with tears and I jumped out of my chair, racing inside, wanting to get as far away as I could from my brush with death.

"Ashley, what happened?" Charlotte called, hurrying after me, her voice filled with concern. "Tell me what happened!"

The tears began falling and then I started to cry. Great big sobs tore from my throat. "The r-r-r-railing. It f-f-f-fell away when I was leaning against it. It fell into the water and then *I* almost fell into the water." I sobbed harder as I realized again what could have happened. "I almost d-d-d-died!"

Charlotte wrapped her arms around me, giving me a reassuring hug. "Shhh. It's okay. You didn't die. You're here. You're safe." She walked me over to my bed and sat me down, reaching for a box of Kleenex on the nightstand between our beds and pulling out a few tissues. She dabbed at my eyes. "I don't understand how something like this could have happened. Doesn't this ship get inspected? Wait until Dad finds out!"

I instantly stopped crying. "No! Don't tell him!" I pleaded, clutching her hands in mine. "Please! He'll only worry and it will freak my mom out."

Charlotte gave me a skeptical look. "Is that the only reason?"

Charlotte clearly guessed what my real reason was. If my parents heard what had happened, they might want me to come home. Even though the ship's staff was supposed to be keeping an eye on us, we really didn't have any chaperones with us. Well, technically, Charlotte was our unofficial chaperone because she was eighteen and so mature—all the parents trusted her to make sure we wouldn't turn into *Teens Gone Wild!*—but I didn't want to chance having my birthday cruise cut short. It was only Day One! It had barely gotten started!

"It was a freak accident," I said, blowing my nose. "That's all."

Charlotte looked at me closely. "Are you sure?"

I nodded, wondering what I had ever done without her. She was acting like a big sister. Until today, she had never really had a reason to. I liked it. A lot.

"Okay. If that's what you want." She gave

me another hug. "But we definitely need to tell someone on board," she said, reaching for the phone.

Ten minutes later the ship sent a maintenance crew. Charlotte and I watched as they inspected the gaping space where the railing had been and the two other sides that it had been attached to, but they didn't come up with any answers. They figured that the bolts holding the railing to the two other sides must have somehow gotten loose. They told us that the salt in the seawater was known to corrode and cause damage, so exposure to the elements could have been a factor.

Another theory was that the bolts had been loosened by hand, but that was quickly dismissed.

"Loosened?" Charlotte laughed, after the men had left. They would be returning the following morning with a new railing. In the meantime, they had told us not to use the outside balcony. That was fine with me. I was planning to never set foot on it again. "Who would have loosened the bolts? If that happened, it wasn't an accident.

It was attempted murder."

Hearing the word *murder* made my blood turn cold.

Then it made me think of Taylor Morton.

Which, of course, made me think of Logan.

But what was I thinking? How could he have slipped into my cabin and loosened the bolts of my railing? That was impossible! Besides, he had no idea I would go out onto the balcony after I left him. It wasn't like he *lured* me out there and said, "Hey, Ashley, lean out over the railing and take a look at that star."

Besides, Logan had no reason to want to hurt me. I hadn't even felt at all threatened when he left me. But . . .

I *had* felt threatened by . . . Finn.

When he stormed out of my cabin, he said I would regret breaking up with him. And his cold stare sent a chill down my spine.

I had been scared of him.

If the bolts *had* been loosened, could Finn have been the one to do it?

I couldn't believe what I was thinking! This was Finn! *Finn!* The guy I had been dating for the last eight months. I'd never been afraid of him before today. Okay, so he had scared me *a little*, and he *was* a practical joker, but that didn't mean he was capable of something so drastic.

I was letting my imagination play tricks on me.

What had happened on the balcony tonight had been an accident. Nothing more.

"I don't know about you, but I'm exhausted," Charlotte said, reaching into a drawer for a nightshirt and heading into the bathroom to get ready for bed.

I wanted to ask Charlotte how the rest of her night with Sam had gone, but I was too tired. I would ask her in the morning. I slipped into my pajamas and fell into bed, leaving my clothes in a pile on the floor. I knew they'd wrinkle, but I didn't care. That's why they make irons. All of a sudden my body was craving sleep. A good night's sleep would help me see clearly and get rid of all these crazy thoughts in my head. I yawned and felt my eyelids starting to droop. Once this horrible day was over, tomorrow would be here, and then my birthday cruise would really kick off! All the bad stuff would be behind me.

I yawned one last time, burrowing my head into my pillow, and then fell asleep.

The next morning I woke up grumpy. I hadn't slept well. I'd been plagued with nightmares, each and every one the same. In my dreams, I hadn't regained my balance. Instead, I had fallen off the deck into the ocean below, my arms and legs flailing before hitting the water.

I woke up every time I hit the water, my heart racing, clutching the sheets against my chest until I gradually realized I was safe in my bed. Luckily, I didn't wake Charlotte. She slept in the bed next to mine, blissfully unaware of what was going on. I would fall back against my mattress, twisting and turning, trying to get comfortable until finally I would drift off to sleep, only to be jolted awake again as I hit the icy water below.

I gave up sleeping at seven A.M., deciding to get an early start on my day. I washed my face and brushed my teeth, pulled my hair into a ponytail, then slipped into a pink T-shirt, white shorts, and sneakers. After that I left a note for

Charlotte and went for breakfast. I was on the Fiesta Deck, checking out the breakfast buffet, trying to decide whether or not I should have bacon or sausage with my scrambled eggs, when a pair of hands covered my eyes.

"Guess who?" a voice whispered in my ear.

I recognized the voice. But I was surprised.

"Logan?"

He removed his hands and I turned around.

"Hi," I said.

"Hi," he said back, sounding kind of shy. "You're up early."

"I didn't have a good night's sleep," I told him, wondering why he had covered my eyes. Or why he was even talking to me. He'd made it sound like he planned to keep his distance from me.

"How come?"

I told him what had happened after I left him. As I did, I could see the shock wash over his face.

"That's awful!" he said. "I'm glad you're okay."

"Really?" I asked the question not because I doubted him but because I had a feeling he had something else that he wanted to say. Something that he wanted me to hear.

"Yes, really." Logan stared at his sneakers. Then he looked up at me. "There's also something I wanted to tell you."

"What?"

"I'm sorry."

"For what?" I asked, genuinely perplexed. What was he apologizing for?

"I'm sorry I jumped to conclusions last night. I'm sorry I doubted you. I should have heard you out. There are two sides to every story."

"You don't have anything to apologize for," I said, turning back to my dish and deciding on the bacon. I added two slices and then went to a table. Logan followed. As I sat down, a waiter brought me a glass of freshly squeezed orange juice. I took a sip. "I don't blame you for getting angry," I told Logan. *Finn* was the one I blamed!

"There's something you should know," Logan said, sitting down next to me. "You were right. There was another girl. My heart was broken last summer. On this very ship. It was a messy breakup. I thought I was over it, but I guess I'm still dealing with it."

I wondered, as I busied myself with buttering my toast, if he was going to bring up Taylor's name. I didn't think it was my place to do it. Besides, I never asked guys about their exes, so why should Logan be any different? If he wanted to tell me about Taylor, he would. In his own time.

"I just wanted to let you know that when I thought things over, I realized I hadn't been fair to you," Logan continued. "You told me the truth. I should have listened. I should have believed you and not Finn. So, can we start over?"

"I'd really like that," I said.

Logan's face lit up. "Great! Want to hang out this afternoon?"

"Sure," I said, taking a bite of my toast and wondering what Logan would want to do. He seemed to like winging it, which I have to admit intrigued me.

I like guys who are hard to figure out.

They present a challenge. And I *loved* challenges!

Logan couldn't stay while I ate my breakfast—
he had to go set things up at the smoothie bar—
but I was going to stop by his cabin at twelve
o'clock. I was so glad he wasn't mad at me
anymore.

After I finished eating I decided to go work
out. Back home I usually went to the gym four
times a week. Going to the gym is *not* one of my
favorite things to do, but I do it for two reasons.
The first is because it's good for me. The second,
and more important reason (at least to me—and
let's admit it, to most people) is to fit into my
size-four wardrobe!

At eight A.M., the gym was pretty much
deserted. But there were two people I didn't
expect to see working out so early.

Sam.

And Finn.

I didn't wave or say good morning to either
one of them. At the same time, I didn't pretend
not to see them. Both were busy. Finn was

working out with a set of weights, as was Sam. Neither one had seen me arrive.

Finn looked like he knew what he was doing with the weights. He practically lived at the gym. But poor Sam didn't have a clue. He was grunting and groaning as he tried to lift a set of weights that were way too heavy for him. They looked like two guys in a BEFORE and AFTER ad for a gym. Hopefully, Sam wouldn't hurt himself.

I hopped on a treadmill, turned on my iPod, and started walking. After half an hour, I did fifty push-ups and sit-ups and then worked out with a set of fifteen-pound hand weights.

After an hour I felt all sore and achey. I hadn't worked out in a week and I was feeling the effects. But it was a good soreness and it let me know that my body was benefiting from all my hard work.

Instead of jumping into the shower, I decided I'd relax in the sauna. It would be a good way to unwind and it would give me some time to think about Logan. Of course, once Kristine and Simone woke up, I'd have to get their thoughts on the whole situation. I still wasn't sure if I was going to tell them about the railing incident. It would only scare them, and by this point I'd pretty much convinced myself it had been nothing but an accident.

I went to the ladies' locker room, slipped out of my clothes, and wrapped myself in a white fluffy towel. Then I pinned up my hair and went into the ladies' sauna.

I was the only one there so I had my pick of seats. I decided to sit on a bench against a far wall.

The heat instantly wrapped itself around me, feeling good against my sore muscles. The steam was thick and growing thicker. I held my hand up in front of me and couldn't see it.

After twenty minutes, I decided that I'd had enough. As soothing as the heat was, I was starting to feel a little light-headed and when that happened I knew it was time to leave.

I left the bench and walked over to the sauna door, pushing against it. It didn't budge.

I pushed again.

And again.

But the door remained shut.

I used two hands, thinking maybe the

door was heavier than I thought, although it hadn't seemed very heavy when I pulled it open earlier.

As I struggled with the door, I became more aware of the heat. It felt like a heavy cloak, wrapping itself around me and squeezing tight, making it harder and harder to breathe.

I wiped at the sweat dripping off my forehead. It was hot, way hot. Hotter than I remembered it being when I first came in. My throat felt like sandpaper and I was craving an ice-cold glass of water.

I kept pushing and pushing against the door. All I wanted to do was get out, but the door still wouldn't open.

Chapter 6

I tried not to panic.

I tried to remain calm.

I took a deep breath and attempted to figure out what was going on.

Obviously, the door was stuck.

I gave it a good push again, but it still wouldn't budge.

What was wrong with it?

I began pounding on the door with my fists, sticking my face in front of the small square pane of glass that was in the center of the door. Suddenly, I was frantic to get out. "Hey!" I shouted as loudly as I could. "Hey! Let me out! Somebody let me out!"

I anxiously listened for the sound of running footsteps, but none came. Where was everyone? Were they stuffing themselves at the all-you-could-eat buffets? Didn't anyone on this ship believe in physical fitness?

I could hear the sound of hissing steam getting louder and louder. *Could you die in a sauna?* I wondered. What would happen if I was trapped in here for hours?

Stop it! I scolded myself. Someone was going to find me. Or I was going to find a way out myself.

I began searching the sauna for something I could use to break the glass in the door. If I did, the steam would flow out into the gym and it would cool off in there. Of course, it was hard to see anything, the steam was so heavy. And even if I did find something to break the glass, would it? It looked like it was really thick. That's probably why no one could hear me.

But what if the glass didn't break?

No, it *would*.

I'd make sure of it.

I searched around the sauna as best as I could, exploring the surfaces that I touched. But I couldn't find anything to break the glass. I returned to the door and did the only thing I could do. I started pounding again.

"Is anyone out there?" I shouted, beating on the door with both fists. I pressed my ear against it, listening for any sort of sound as I continued to pound. "Help me! Please! Help me!"

I kept yelling as loudly as I could, but my voice was becoming hoarse. My arms were also getting tired. I didn't know how much longer I could keep pounding. My entire body felt limp. Was I getting dehydrated with each gulp of hot, steamy air?

And then it happened.

Finally, the door opened.

As it did, the steam wafted out and cool air flowed in. I raced toward it, escaping the hotness of the sauna. I must have stumbled because I almost fell. But a pair of strong hands caught me, leading me to a nearby bench.

"Ashley?"

It was Sam. What was he doing here?

"What happened?" he asked, helping me to sit.

"I was trapped in there. I thought I was going to die. But you saved me. Thanks."

Sam laughed. It was an annoying, condescending laugh and it made me angry.

"What's so funny?" I snapped.

"I don't think you were going to die. You would have had to have been in there a lot longer and at a much higher temperature."

"How do you know?"

"I just do." He then started giving me some chemistry lecture that I *didn't* need to hear. I held up a hand. "Enough!"

He stopped talking. Then he walked over to a water fountain and filled a paper cup. "Here," he said, offering me the water. "Drink this."

I grabbed the cup out of his hand, bringing it to my parched lips, and emptying it in seconds. I held it out to him, wanting more. He went and refilled it, bringing it back to me.

I took a small sip this time. The icy coldness of the water tasted *so* good! And the gym's air-conditioning was cooling me off. The feeling of light-headedness I had experienced only moments before was disappearing.

"Why couldn't I get out?" I asked.

Sam pointed to a hand truck that was

stacked with boxes of Italian tiles. "That hand truck was pressed against the door. Someone must have left it there and then gone off to do something else."

"That was pretty careless!"

"I'm sure whoever it was would have eventually come back."

"How did you know I was in there?"

"I was finishing up my workout when I heard pounding. So I came back here to see what was going on. You're lucky I took off my iPod and found you. The gym's deserted. Who knows how long you could have been in there?"

"Thanks again for letting me out," I said, getting to my feet. I must have gotten up too fast, because suddenly I swayed. I thought I was going to fall, but Sam's arms wrapped around me, helping me to sit back down.

"Are you sure you're okay?" he asked. "Maybe we should get you checked out by a doctor."

Sam began looking around the gym, as if hoping a doctor would miraculously appear. Then I noticed something. Sam was keeping his eyes averted from me. He was also red in the face and it *wasn't* from his workout.

Sam was embarrassed!

I looked down at myself and realized why. I was wearing a thin towel and it clung to my body. But why was he looking away? Usually, I felt like Sam was studying me. Now, when he had the opportunity, he wasn't. Obviously, he wasn't checking me out the way most guys would check out a scantily clad girl. So why did I always feel like I was under a microscope with him? What was going on in that head of his?

I was too exhausted from my extended sauna to try and figure things out. Sam had saved me and that was all that mattered.

Sam handed me a terrycloth robe hanging on the wall behind us. "Here, put this on. That towel is drenched."

"Thanks." I belted the robe around myself. "I guess you're my hero today."

"Any time."

I started to walk back to the locker room.

"So I hear you have a new boyfriend," he called out after me. "Is it that guy you introduced me and Charlotte to last night? What was his name again? Logan? I thought you wanted to take some time off from dating. Isn't that what you said yesterday?"

My head whipped around. "Who told you I have a new boyfriend?"

"Your *ex*-boyfriend. He didn't seem too happy about it."

"When did he tell you?"

"This morning. Didn't you see him? He was working off a lot of steam." Sam laughed. "That's kind of funny. He was working off steam and you were trapped in steam."

I ignored Sam's joke. "Logan's not my boyfriend. He's just a friend."

"Finn says it didn't look that way when you were having breakfast this morning."

"Is he *spying* on me?" I exploded.

Sam shrugged. "Beats me. But he was mad. *Really* mad. If I were you, I'd watch my back."

"What do you mean?"

"Finn kept saying he was going to get even with you, teach you a lesson. I don't know what he meant, but I'm sure it's not going to be good."

I didn't know what to say to Sam—I guess I was in shock—so I left the gym and headed back to my cabin to take a shower. When I got there, I saw that Charlotte was already gone. She was probably playing in a shuffleboard tournament or learning how to salsa or whatever cruise directors are supposed to do to keep you entertained. Our cruise director was Kayla and she was a perky brunette with tons of energy. Every time I saw her, she was running around like crazy with her megaphone, making announcements and trying to get people to sign up for different activities and tournaments.

Since Charlotte wasn't in the cabin, I decided to take as much time as I liked in the shower (although I kept the water at a tepid temperature. I'd had enough hot steam and heat in my life for one day!). Even though Logan and I didn't officially have a date, I wanted to make sure I looked my best.

But as I went through my first-date ritual of showering, shampooing, and conditioning, I kept thinking of Sam's words. And it got me to wondering.

Could Finn have been the one to trap me in the sauna? Maybe he *had* seen me come into the gym. And maybe *he* had been the one to put that stack of tiles against the sauna door.

First the balcony and now this.

Were they just both weird coincidences?

Or did I need to watch my back like Sam said?

After I got out of the shower, I wrapped my hair in a towel, turban-style, and headed to my closet to pick out an outfit. It needed to look casual and quickly tossed together, yet also slightly chic. I didn't want Logan thinking I'd planned what I was going to wear, even though I had.

I went through my hangers, pulling out different tops, skirts, shorts, and jeans, and with each second I found myself getting angry. I'd never been afraid of Finn before and I wasn't going to start now.

I was going to put an end to this.

I decided to wear a white embroidered eyelet top, a pair of black capris, and braided-leather sandals. After a quick blow-dry, I pushed my hair off my forehead with a black headband and accessorized with a pair of silver hoop earrings and a silver charm bracelet, tucking a silver-and-gold patchwork clutch under one arm.

Before leaving the cabin I checked myself out in the full-length mirror behind our door and loved what I saw, hoping Logan would too. Then I went off in search of Finn.

He was sitting by the pool, the first place I thought to look for him. For someone who had recently been dumped, he didn't look very broken-hearted.

That's because Tabitha was sharing his chaise lounge, sitting on his lap, and applying suntan lotion to his arms and shoulders. It was taking longer than it should, but maybe that's because Tabitha was spending an unnecessary amount of time massaging his biceps and simultaneously kissing him. And not small, tiny kisses, but deep open-mouthed kisses with tongue action. Was this public display of affection really necessary? I wondered.

It was the first time I was seeing Tabitha since we'd gotten on the ship. I hated to admit it, but she looked good, *very* good. But that was no surprise. When it came to clothes and putting herself together, Tabby knew what she was doing. She was *almost* as good as me.

Today she was wearing a white one-piece

swimsuit with cut-out sides—the better to show off her already golden-brown tan—and a plunging front, along with cork wedge sandals and a huge pair of black sunglasses. Her shoulder-length brunette hair fell in cascading waves that had that casual windblown look that always looked like messy bed-head on me.

"I want to talk to you," I said to Finn.

Finn stopped kissing Tabitha and stared at me over her shoulder. He was wearing mirrored sunglasses and I couldn't see his eyes. "About what?"

"Don't play dumb. You know what."

"I don't," he said. "So will you please stop talking in riddles and just tell me what you want? Tabitha and I are busy."

More like *getting* busy!

I'm not the kind of girl who judges. If you want to sleep with a guy, fine. For me, it has to mean something and so far I hadn't found the right guy to go all the way with. Finn tried plenty of times with me, but it just never felt right, so I never gave in. I know that frustrated him and he sweet-talked me plenty of times, but

I never changed my mind. I guess, deep down, I knew he wasn't the one.

Tabitha was the complete opposite of me. If she liked a guy and she wanted to go all the way with him, she did. Maybe that's because she claimed to be in love with every guy she was with. It was hard enough for me to find one special guy. She was able to find three in one year?

I'm not judging!

Much.

"What do you want?" Tabitha asked crossly, pushing her sunglasses up on her head and glaring at me. "Can't you come back later?"

I ignored her. "I want you to leave me alone," I told Finn. "Do you understand?"

"What are you talking about?" He glowered at me.

"Your little stunt this morning. In the gym?" I decided not to mention the railing because that could have been a freak accident. But not this. "Locking me in the sauna. I didn't find it very funny."

"Who says I locked you in the sauna?"

"I was there working out the same time as you."

"So? Just because I was there when you were, you're accusing me of something I didn't do?"

"You saw me," I said. "You followed me and then you blocked the door so I couldn't get out. If Sam hadn't found me, who knows how long I would have been trapped in there?"

"You're crazy!" Finn exclaimed, ripping off his sunglasses and showing me his angry blue eyes. "You were still working out when I left the gym so there's no way I could have done what you're saying."

"Really? Then how come you told Sam that I was going to regret breaking up with you?"

"Because you are," Tabitha interjected. "Finn's a great guy and you threw him away." She nestled up against him, kissing the side of his neck. "And now he's mine." She then gave me her *back off* expression where her green eyes narrow into tiny slits and she kind of snarls at you. That face has been known to scare off other girls, but not me.

I resisted rolling my eyes. Please! How

dumb was Tabitha? The only reason Finn was hanging out with her was to make me jealous.

Well, it wasn't going to work.

If Finn wanted Tabby, he could have her. Actually, it would serve him right! Tabitha was the girlfriend from hell. After a month of dating her, Finn would be running for the hills.

"Maybe you should talk to your hero," Finn said.

"Huh?"

"I wasn't the only one working out in the gym the same time as you. Sam was there too. Don't you think it was convenient the way he found you? That guy has a crush on you. He doesn't have the guts to do anything about it, but he likes you."

"Sam doesn't have a crush on me," I said. I'd *never* gotten that vibe from him. When he looked at me, it was a different kind of staring—not the kind of staring a guy did when he was checking you out. "The only girl he's interested in is Charlotte."

"What if I'm right?" Finn suggested. "Maybe *Sam's* the one who locked you in that sauna just so he could rescue you. I bet he'd love to score points with you."

Finn's theory left me speechless.

But I had no proof.

Just Finn's word against Sam's.

Like Sam's word against Finn's.

Were they both innocent?

Or was one of them guilty?

I was so confused!

"Just stay away from me," I told Finn. "It's over between us. Obviously, you've moved on, so we have nothing more to say to each other."

"Except happy birthday," Finn said, putting his sunglasses back on. "See you at your party, Ash. Don't worry, I won't give you a birthday kiss. Tabitha's the only one who's getting my kisses."

"And I can't get enough of them!" She giggled, tossing her arms back around his neck as she locked lips with him.

I turned away, wishing I could uninvite both Finn and Tabitha to my party.

Chapter 7

*A*fter leaving the Gruesome Twosome, I headed to Logan's cabin, wondering what plans he had up his sleeve. I hoped it was something fun because I was ready to have a good time.

Logan's cabin was on the second-to-last deck of the ship. When I got off the elevator to search for it, I passed a lot of people wearing uniforms. This was probably the deck where the staff stayed.

Finally, I found cabin 226 and knocked on the door. Butterflies were dancing around in my stomach. I was nervous. I wanted Logan to like me. I didn't want to ruin this second chance. I wanted him to get to know the *real* me.

Seconds later the door opened and I saw something I didn't expect.

It was Logan. Wearing nothing but a white

towel wrapped snugly around his waist!

"Sorry, I'm running late," he explained as I entered his cabin. It was small, way smaller than my cabin. It wasn't even as big as my walk-in closet at home. There was a twin bed, dresser, and closet, along with a tiny bathroom.

"I had a little accident with the blender," Logan explained. "I thought I had the lid on tight but I got splashed all over with a blueberry smoothie." I noticed some purpley blue globs in his hair.

"Maybe you were too busy checking out your customer and that's why you forgot," I teased. "You got distracted."

Logan pretended to think. "Funny, I don't remember you ordering a blueberry smoothie this morning."

"Sweet talker."

"It'll only take me a couple of minutes to rinse off and get dressed," he promised. "Then we can go."

Even though I was listening to Logan's explanation, I wasn't *really* listening. I was too busy checking out his body. There's a difference between checking out a guy from a distance and then seeing him up close. Logan was in *great* shape.

And wearing so little!

I tried not to stare, but it was hard.

I've always been attracted to guys who take care of themselves. Of course, what's inside matters most, but let's be honest, packaging gets a girl's attention too! I know it's not fair, but it's true.

We were standing so close together, there was hardly any space between us. If I'd wanted to, I could have reached out and touched Logan.

But I didn't.

I wanted to, but it felt too soon. We hadn't even gone out on a first date!

I eased past him and sat down on his bed. "Take your time," I offered. "No rush."

He gave me a smile and I melted. "Thanks!"

While he was in the shower, I walked around the tiny cabin. Like most guys I knew, Logan wasn't very neat. There were used towels, T-shirts, pairs of dirty socks, sneakers, and sandals tossed on the floor; piles of magazines and DVDs were stacked on top of the dresser.

I flipped through the DVDs, curious to see what kind of movies he liked. There were a lot of comedies, like *American Pie, Harold and Kumar Go to White Castle, Blades of Glory,* and *Borat*. There were also a bunch of superhero movies like *Spider-Man, Fantastic Four,* and the *X-Men* trilogy.

As I flipped through the DVDs, I noticed a camera on top of the dresser. It wasn't digital but a camera that used film. It looked expensive. Next to the camera was a pile of photographs. The photo on top caught my eye and I couldn't resist picking it up.

It was a girl around the same age as me. The photo was a close-up, so a lot of details jumped out at me. She had brown hair streaked with blond highlights, and brown eyes with thick lashes. There was also a scattering of freckles across her nose and cheek.

But that wasn't what I noticed most.

It was the thin gold necklace around her neck.

It had a nameplate that I could read.

Taylor.

A jolt of shock went through me.

I was staring at Taylor Morton.

This was the girl who had disappeared last summer.

The girl who Logan had dated.

The girl he had fought with before her disappearance.

A girl who was probably dead.

I dropped the photo like it was a hot coal. Until a few seconds ago, Taylor Morton had only been a name to me.

Now she had a face.

And that made her real.

I grabbed the remote control sitting on the dresser and aimed it at the TV, trying to focus on the movie that came on the screen.

But I couldn't.

Why did Logan still have a photo of Taylor? I wondered. What was it a reminder of?

Just then Logan emerged from the bathroom wearing a pair of black running shorts. His hair was wet and slicked back. Droplets of water were scattered over his shoulders and chest.

He opened up a dresser drawer and took out a lime-green tank top, pulling it over his head.

"Sorry my cabin is such a mess," he said as he sat down on his bed and yanked on a pair of sneakers. "I'm not big on neatness."

"That's okay." I pointed to the camera. "Are you a photographer?"

He nodded. "Yeah, I like taking pictures. Sometimes I use my bathroom as a darkroom. Yesterday I found a roll of film that I had taken last summer and developed it. I had left it in my suitcase and forgotten all about it. I found it when I was looking for some clean socks."

So that explained it!

"Are those the photos?" I asked, pointing to the pile on the dresser. "Can I look at them?"

Logan shrugged. "Sure."

I started flipping through the pictures. There were a lot of photos of the islands. Of sunrises and sunsets. Tropical birds and flowers.

And Taylor.

"Who's this?" I asked, waving a photo of Taylor, hoping my question sounded casual. I didn't know how to bring up the subject of Taylor and I figured I would let Logan tell me whatever he wanted to.

A look of sadness washed over Logan's face. "Someone I used to know," he said, his voice low and hoarse.

"Someone special?"

I don't know why I asked the question, but I wanted to know what Taylor had meant to Logan. That might be selfish of me, but every girl wants to know if an ex-girlfriend still has a place in her old boyfriend's heart. Although Finn and I were finished, I did have a few sweet memories. Like the time he bought me a stuffed puppy when I was out sick with the flu, popping the puppy around the corner of my bedroom door and talking to me like Scooby-Doo. Or the time he waited in line in the rain for two hours at Madison Square Garden to get me tickets to a Beyoncé concert because he knew how much I loved her.

Logan shook his head. "Just someone I used to know."

Okay. He didn't want to talk about her. I wasn't going to push. He'd tell me when he was ready.

I abandoned the photos and joined Logan

on his bed. We were sitting so close together, our arms and legs were touching. The butterflies in my stomach came back, only this time they weren't nervous butterflies. I was excited. I liked being so close to him.

"What did you do this morning?" he asked.

I decided not to tell Logan about my experience in the sauna. First the railing and then the sauna. I didn't want him thinking I was some sort of klutz. "I worked out."

"Maybe we can work out together later in the week," he suggested.

"And have you see me all sweaty?" I asked in horror. I shook my head firmly. "I don't think so." I pointed to his camera. "How long have you been taking pictures?"

"Since I was ten. My grandfather gave me a camera for my birthday. I try to take it with me everywhere."

"I bet your sisters love that."

Logan gave an evil Bart Simpson chuckle. "I've caught them on film plenty of times when they've had their hair in hot rollers, faces slathered with mud masks, and puffy pillow faces when they've just gotten up."

"Oh, you're bad!"

Logan jumped off the bed and grabbed his camera. "Pose for me."

"What?"

"Pose for me! Pretend you're a contestant on *America's Next Top Model*."

I shrieked. "Don't tell me you watch that show too?!"

"Two older sisters," Logan reminded me as he aimed his camera in my direction. "Plus, the girls are hot!"

I jumped off the bed and began posing. At first I was serious, but then I started making silly faces, trying to get Logan to laugh. He did. And then he started talking in a fake French accent.

"Zee photos, zay are magnifique! You are zee most beautiful model on zee show!"

Finally, when Logan ran out of film, we collapsed on the bed, laughing, our faces close together.

"You know, there's something I've been wanting to do since I first met you," he confessed.

"What?" I asked.

"This," he said as he pressed his lips against mine.

Logan's kiss was totally unexpected. I knew he liked me, but I didn't think he'd make the first move so fast!

His kiss was nice. Very nice. It started out slow and soft and quickly heated up. Goose bumps traveled through my body and I began to feel tingly all over, especially when Logan's lips broke away from mine and he began kissing the side of my neck, his hands moving up and down my arms and shoulders. Then he leaned against the headboard of his bed, pulling me to him. I liked being nestled in his arms.

"How about we stay in the cabin this afternoon?" he asked, nuzzling my ear.

"And do what?" I asked, my breath catching in my throat. "Take more pictures?"

"This," he said, leaning down to give me another kiss, one that was longer and deeper, one hand trailing down my back.

I have to admit, I was tempted. But things were moving a little too fast for me. I wanted to get to know Logan a little bit better. And

I didn't want him to expect anything I wasn't ready to do.

I kissed him back, trying to make the kiss last as long as possible, and then jumped off the bed. "I'm starving. Let's get something to eat. We can always come back later."

"Promise?" he playfully asked. "We can develop that film and find your cover photo for next month's issue of *Vogue*."

"With an offer like that, how could I refuse?"

There were lots of restaurants on the ship. I didn't care where we ate. I just wanted to spend time with Logan and get to know him better. He suggested we go to Harry's Hula Hut, which was on the Fiesta Deck and had a Hawaiian theme. The inside of the restaurant was decorated to look like an island hut, with lots of bamboo and wicker furniture, palm trees, and ceiling fans. The waitresses all wore grass skirts with coconut bras, and leis around their necks, while the waiters wore white shorts and short-sleeved shirts with tropical designs.

We were given a table that looked out on the water. Much to my disappointment, I could see dark clouds brewing in the distance. That meant no lounging by the pool after lunch.

Logan noticed the frown on my face and followed my gaze. "These storms don't last very long. An hour or two, tops. Then the sun comes right out." He reached across the table for my hand. "Don't worry. You'll be able to show off your bikini for me."

"How did you know I was going to wear a bikini?" I asked, picking up my menu and pretending to read it. "Maybe I was going to wear a one-piece today."

Logan shook his head. "You're not a one-piece girl. You know you look hot in a bikini. That's the first thing I noticed about you yesterday."

I put the menu down. "It is? What else did you notice?"

"Your smile. It lights up your whole face."

"Your smile's not so bad, either," I admitted.

"So you like my smile, huh?" He gave me a grin. "What else do you like about me?"

Before I could answer, our waitress arrived to take our order. It was Molly, the waitress I'd met the night before.

"Hey, you two!" she exclaimed. "First date?"

"I didn't know you were working here today," Logan said.

I noticed he hadn't answered her question.

"What can I say? I had an irresistible urge to wear a grass skirt," she said, swiveling her hips. "At least it's better than working in the Bistro."

"That's the French restaurant on the Panama Deck," Logan explained to me.

"If you work in the Bistro, you have to wear an off-the-shoulder black-and-white striped shirt," she said.

"And a beret!" Logan added.

Molly shuddered. "*Hate* the beret!"

"Every week they rotate us among the different restaurants on the ship," Logan told me. "You never know where you're going to end up."

"But you're guaranteed to be wearing a wacky uniform," Molly sighed, turning to a clean page on her order pad. "Last week I had to wear a kimono with chopsticks in my hair at the Jade Palace. So, what can I get for you two?"

I ordered a tropical fruit salad. Logan went for a cheeseburger and fries. After giving Molly his order he realized he had forgotten his wallet and went back to his cabin to get it, leaving us alone.

"I'm glad you're going out with him," Molly said.

"We're not dating," I answered instantly.

"It looks like a date to me."

"Does it?" I wanted some sort of reassurance. It *did* feel like a date to me, but Logan hadn't confirmed it when Molly asked. To me, that meant he didn't think of it as a date. But he was acting like it was. So was it? Guys were so hard to figure out sometimes! And he *had* kissed me. More than once!

Molly sat down in the seat across from me. "Can I give you some advice?" She didn't wait for me to answer. "Give him some time. Go slow. He's scared."

"Scared?" That wasn't what I had expected to hear. "Of what?"

"Of getting hurt again," she explained. "Taylor really did a number on him last year. He thought she was serious about him and she wasn't."

"How do you know that?"

"Logan and I are friends. This will be our second summer working together, but we keep in touch during the year. It's hard for him to open up, but that's the case with most guys. Eventually, they'll tell you things in bits and pieces until you get the whole story."

"I haven't asked him about Taylor," I told Molly. "It's none of my business. I figure if he wants to tell me, he will."

At that moment, Logan came back to the table, ending our conversation. "What are you two whispering about?"

Molly got out of Logan's seat. "We were talking about what you could do this afternoon since it doesn't look like you'll be heading out to the pool any time soon."

While Logan had been gone it had started raining, and big fat drops were splattering against the window.

"I passed the movie theater on my way

back here," he said, sitting down. "How about catching a flick?"

"Sure," I agreed. "What's playing?"

"I think it was a horror movie."

Molly shivered. "I hate those."

"So do I," I admitted.

Logan leaned across the table. "Don't worry, I'll protect you if you get scared," he said, taking my hand in his.

"But horror movies really scare me," I confessed. "I might even jump into your lap."

Logan gave me a smile, only this one was wicked. "*Really*? I wouldn't have a problem with that."

I knew he wouldn't, either.

The movie theater was crowded because of the bad weather.

"Where do you want to sit?" Logan asked.

Since it was a horror movie, I wanted to sit as far away from the screen as possible. The back rows had already filled up but there were still some open seats in the middle.

"Let's snag those," I said, pointing at a row.

As we hurried to our seats, I could see

Kristine and Simone sitting on the other side of the theater. Their mouths dropped open when they saw me with Logan. I gave them a wave and then sat down.

"Want any munchies?" Logan asked.

"Absolutely!"

"What do you like?"

"Popcorn, *no* butter. A box of Raisinets and a Dr. Pepper."

Logan left to buy our snacks. As soon as he was gone, Simone and Kristine raced over. I hadn't seen them all day, so I was glad they had decided to check out a movie too.

Because of the icky weather, Simone and Kristine had both chosen to wear jeans. Kristine had gone for skinny ones while Simone's were low-rise. Kristine had topped her jeans with a paisley top with bell sleeves and Simone was wearing a pink baby T that said *GOOD GIRL GONE BAD* on its front.

"When did you hook up with him?" Simone asked, sounding like she was impressed.

"Why are you hooking up with him?" Kristine asked, her voice filled with worry.

I held up a hand. "We'll dish after the

movie," I said. "Go back to your seats! I don't want him to think we're talking about him."

They both scowled but did as I asked.

Logan got back to his seat just as the house lights went down. He put the bucket of popcorn on the armrest between us and then handed me my soda and box of Raisinets. I promptly opened them and sprinkled them into the popcorn. Logan grimaced. "Gross! Why did you do that?"

"Trust me, they taste delicious together."

Logan reached into the bucket for a handful of the mixture and tossed it into his mouth, chewing slowly. I knew he wanted to make a face, but he didn't.

"Hmm . . . not bad, I guess."

I punched him lightly on the arm. "Told you!"

The opening credits of the movie rolled on the screen and creepy music filled the theater. We were seeing some flick called *Killing Spree* about an eighteen-year-old girl who escapes from a mental institution and starts killing off her sorority sisters. You never get to see the killer's face, so you don't know which one of the new pledges is actually the killer.

I hate horror movies because the directors always try to fool you with fake scares. Like the heroine goes to close a window and her cat jumps inside. That stuff makes me jump out of my seat. *Always.* It used to crack Finn up and he'd tease me about it, saying I should stick with G-rated movies. Once, he even hid in my hall closet and popped out at me when I came back from answering a phone call in the kitchen. At first I thought he had gone to the bathroom but as time passed and he never came back, I called for him. I was standing at the bottom of the staircase that led to our upstairs bathroom, calling out his name, when he grabbed me from behind. I was *so* mad at him that time!

When I'm not jumping out of my seat at horror movies, I'm usually tearing my eyes away from the screen or staring down at the floor or my lap.

The sorority killer hadn't struck yet. She'd just been torturing the heroine with heavy-breathing phone calls and creepy notes. But I knew the body count would start soon. I focused on my bucket of popcorn, and as I reached in my hand bumped Logan's.

Accident? I think not.

"I'm going to go get another soda," Logan whispered, shaking his empty cup at me. "You want anything?"

I shook my head. "I'm okay."

"I'll be right back."

"Hurry," I told him. "You don't want to miss anything."

I also didn't want to be sitting alone. Even though I was surrounded by other people, I felt safer with Logan next to me.

As I continued watching the movie, I suddenly got a creepy feeling.

Someone was *watching* me.

I casually turned in my seat, glancing around the theater. But it was too dark to see anything.

Scary music started to build as one of the sorority sisters started climbing up the stairs to the second floor of the Delta Phi Kappa house, asking if anyone was home. She was so dumb! If I was home alone and I heard a noise, I wouldn't *investigate* — I'd be running out the front door!

But if she didn't go upstairs, there would be no body count. I was pretty sure she was going to be Victim Number One.

I tried to keep my eyes on the screen, ignoring the feeling I'd had. It was probably just my imagination.

But a few minutes later, I felt it again.

It was like a set of eyes were burning into my back.

Stop it, I told myself. *No one is staring at you.*

But the feeling wouldn't go away.

And then I heard it.

A soft voice calling my name.

Ashley...

I had to be imagining it.

But then I heard it again.

Ashhhhleeeee...

It was like the sound of a hissing snake! Goose bumps rose on my arms and my stomach did flip-flops.

People in the audience began calling out. "Shush! Be quiet!"

Who was calling my name? I didn't want to turn around again to find out. I was too afraid.

I watched on the screen as the sorority sister went into the bathroom to take a shower. As she pulled the shower curtain behind her and turned on the water, a shadowy figure started looming. Moving closer and closer.

The scary music continued to build.

Then the shower curtain was pulled back and the sorority sister screamed as a knife plunged toward her.

At that moment, Logan plopped back into his seat. His sudden reappearance caused me to scream and jump up, spilling popcorn and Raisinets everywhere.

"Sorry! I didn't mean to scare you," he said, taking a sip of his soda. "What did I miss?"

For the rest of the movie, I clutched Logan's arm, burying my face in his shoulder whenever the scary music started up. He didn't seem to mind, unlike Finn, who always used to complain that I was wrinkling his shirt. I kept listening for my name being called, but I didn't hear it again. That should have made me feel better, but it didn't. I wanted to know who it had been.

As soon as the movie was over and the lights went back on, I looked around the theater.

Not only were Finn and Tabitha getting out of seats a few rows behind us, but so were Sam and Charlotte.

Staring at Finn and then Sam, I wondered.

Could one of them have been trying to scare me?

Chapter 8

*T*he movie wasn't that scary," Logan said as we walked out of the theater.

"I'd have to disagree," I said, moving closer to him and taking his hand in mine. It was something a girlfriend would do with her boyfriend, but that's not why I did it. Holding Logan's hand made me feel safe, protected. I was still feeling scared and I didn't know why.

I looked over my shoulder and then I knew.

Finn and Sam were both staring at me.

Finn had a smirk on his face. Was it because he knew how badly he had spooked me? He knew I hated horror movies, and he had probably seen Logan leave his seat. Had he been the one whispering my name?

Or had it been Sam?

Sam was looking at me in disbelief, like he couldn't believe I was with another guy. Could Finn have been right? Did he have a crush on me? Had he decided to scare me after seeing me with Logan? But he couldn't have been the one whispering my name. Charlotte had been sitting next to him during the movie.

If I had to choose between the two of them, I'd have to choose Finn as the guilty one. He had more reason to be mad at me.

I didn't know what to think or believe. I just wanted them to leave me alone!

I turned my back on them. As I did, Logan leaned close to me and whispered in my ear, "Want to go back to my cabin?"

There was no mistaking the tone in Logan's voice. He didn't just want to go back to his cabin. He wanted to pick up where we'd left off.

Ordinarily, I wouldn't have a problem with that. I liked Logan. Really, I did. And I liked kissing him—a lot. But there was something else in his voice, something unspoken.

The boy wanted to do more than just kiss; I could sense it.

I instantly dropped his hand. Had I been

sending the wrong signals? My eyes fell on a dry-erase board listing the ship's activities for the day. A fashion show was starting in ten minutes at the Paris Boutique.

"I can't." I pointed to the board. "I'm going to the fashion show with my friends Simone and Kristine." Okay, it was a lie, but a little white lie. I couldn't tell Logan the real reason why I didn't want to go back to his cabin.

"But you promised that we'd go back," he said. He sounded like a little boy who'd been expecting dessert if he cleaned his dinner plate.

"I know I did. But . . ."

But what?

How did I explain it to him?

I didn't want this to be just about sex. I wanted something more with Logan.

This time I was going to do what I wanted to do. Finn had always called the shots, and whenever I didn't want to do something, he would guilt me into it. No more!

"I forgot that I made plans with Simone and Kristine."

"Can't you break them?" He made a sad face. "For me?"

His sad face was near irresistible, but I couldn't be tempted.

"I can't. It wouldn't be right. I'm not the kind of girl who ditches her friends when she meets a new guy."

"Well, I guess I understand, with you being so into fashion and all. And I like that you're loyal to your friends. I just didn't want our first date to end."

"Date?" I was surprised by his words. "This was a date?"

"Wasn't it?"

I shrugged. "I thought we were just hanging out," I said, echoing his words from earlier in the day. "I mean, you never *officially* asked me out. I didn't want to assume anything, you know?"

"Friends who hang out don't do this," he said, turning to face me and then pressing his lips against mine.

Logan's kiss was hungry and fierce. It was a kiss filled with desire. He wanted to be with me. He was making that very clear.

As he continued to kiss me, I wondered if I was making a mistake. Maybe we could take things slow. Maybe . . .

Logan broke the kiss, ending all my sweet sensations. "Enjoy your fashion show," he said. "I'll see you later."

I watched him walk away. Part of me wanted to run after him, grab him by the hand, and drag him to his cabin. Those lips were powerful! But I didn't. I broke free of the spell I had fallen under and stuck to my original decision.

But I'd need to be more careful next time. Logan's kisses were dangerous!

"Having a shipboard romance?" an ugly voice asked me. I whirled around and saw Finn standing behind me, a sneer on his face. I could tell he was angry just from the way his body was coiled with tension. I looked around for Tabitha but didn't see her anywhere.

"I'm surprised he still has two arms," he said. "You were holding on to him so tight during the movie."

So he *had* been watching me!

And he'd probably been the one whispering my name. He knew how easily I got scared at horror movies. But if I accused him, he'd never admit to it. So I wasn't going to.

"I don't have to answer your questions," I

told him. "Who I go out with is none of your business." I was *so* over this. "Go away, Finn. You're with Tabitha now and I'm with Logan."

"You heard her," Simone said, walking up behind me. "Get lost!"

"Beat it!" Kristine added as she came to stand on the other side of me.

Finn scowled at the three of us before leaving without another word.

"What's his problem?" I asked after he was gone.

"Jealousy," Simone said. "He's a sore loser."

"Enough about Finn!" Kristine said. "He's ancient history. What's going on with you and Logan? My eyes nearly popped out of my head when I saw you walk into the movie theater with him."

"We've started hanging out together," I said.

"You've been doing *more* than just hanging out," Simone said. "Don't think we didn't see that kiss!"

"It wasn't the first kiss," I admitted, feeling my cheeks turn red. I knew I was blushing.

"What?!" Simone exclaimed. "You need to bring us up to speed. From the very beginning!"

"Okay, but let's go to the fashion show at the Paris Boutique. It's going to start any second."

"Why do you want to go to the fashion show?" Kristine asked.

I pointed to a porthole and the rain that was still coming down. "We can't do anything outside. And when Logan asked me to go back to his cabin, I used going to the fashion show with you as an excuse. He wasn't too happy about it, but things got a little too heavy when we were in his cabin earlier."

"You've *already* been in his cabin?" Simone gasped, staring at me like I was a stranger. "Girl, what else have you been up to since the last time we saw you?"

"Don't look so shocked," I said as I started walking to the nearest elevator. "I'll fill you in during the fashion show."

A speechless Simone and Kristine hurried after me.

The fashion show was fabulous. There were so many one-of-a-kind outfits I wanted to buy.

I'm not one of those shopaholic types, but a girl can never have too many clothes. Before leaving for the cruise, my father told me that because it was my birthday, I could do a little shopping if I saw anything I really *had* to have. I've never abused Daddy's credit cards, and Charlotte didn't even use hers.

On our way to the fashion show, we ran into Charlotte and I asked her if she wanted to join us, but she couldn't. She and Sam were going to play in a Scrabble tournament. She did ask me, though, to keep an eye out for anything I thought she might like.

When the fashion show ended, the outfits we had seen were brought out on racks so we could go through them. I already knew which ones I wanted to try on. The first was a black lace dress with a ribbon belt and the second was a peach slip dress with tiny pearl buttons down the front. I'd also seen a bright yellow baby-doll dress that I thought would look great on Charlotte. Simone had picked a red dress with spaghetti straps to try on while Kristine had chosen a lilac tank dress and a forest-green micromini skirt.

As we explored the racks, Simone and Kristine bombarded me with questions. During the fashion show I had told them about the time I'd spent with Logan. The only things I left out were the loose railing and my sauna scare. I wanted to forget about the trauma and just have fun.

"You're not afraid to be with him?" Kristine asked as she stood in front of a full-length mirror and held a fitted white jacket up against her chest. "You know? Because of Taylor?"

"We talked about this last night," I told Kristine sternly, taking the white jacket out of her hands and replacing it with one that was much cuter. "No charges were filed against him. It's not fair to judge him. He's a nice guy and he didn't have anything to do with Taylor's disappearance. I feel perfectly safe when I'm with him."

"Okay," Kristine said. "Message received loud and clear."

I gave Kristine a smile. I knew she was only looking out for me. That's what best friends did.

If there was anyone I should be afraid of, it

was Finn. He was the one who was scaring me.

As we walked to the dressing room to try on our outfits, I spied a silver-beaded dress on a rack. It had been the last dress modeled in the show and I loved the way the lights glittered off it. It was so sparkly and shiny—the perfect dress to wear to my birthday party!

As I reached for the dress, so did someone on the other side of the rack.

Tabitha.

"I saw it first," she said, tightening her grip on the hanger.

If I had been anyone else, Tabitha probably would have given up the dress. But because it was me, she wouldn't budge.

"I picked it up *first*, Tabby," I said, tightening my own grip.

"You did not," she insisted, her red lips pursing with determination. "I did."

"Why don't you let go of the dress, Tabitha?" Kristine asked. "You know it's going to look much better on Ashley than it would on you."

Oooh! *Wrong* thing to say! Tabitha's grip on

the dress tightened even more.

"Is that a mouse?" Simone gasped, pointing to the floor by Tabitha's feet and running away.

Tabitha shrieked, letting go of the dress and jumping up on a footstool.

"Where? Where?" she cried, hugging her arms against herself. "Where is it?"

"My eyes must have been playing tricks on me," Simone said with a smirk as she walked back, giving me a wink. She shrugged. "I guess I was wrong. That dress is going to look fabulous on you, Ashley. Let's go try it on."

Tabitha's eyes narrowed into two nasty slits. If looks could kill, I would've been dead.

I bought the silver dress. If Tabby had really wanted it, I would have given it to her. But she had stormed out of the boutique before I could say anything. I felt guilty but not *too* guilty. The dress looked good on me, and I couldn't wait to pair it with the perfect shoes and accessories.

After charging the purchases to my cabin,

I decided to take my outfits back to my room. (I bought everything I had tried on and also bought the yellow baby-doll dress for Charlotte.) Kristine, who bought a new bikini, and Simone, who was the proud owner of a slamming new micromini skirt, were going to do the same thing. We made plans to meet in fifteen minutes at the Roasted Bean, a coffee bar on the Diablo Deck.

On the way to my cabin, I wondered where Logan was. I missed him. I know that sounds strange, but I was dying to get to know him better.

The first thing I did when I got back to my cabin was drop my bags on top of my bed. The salesgirl at the boutique did such a great job wrapping everything in tissue paper, I wasn't afraid of stuff wrinkling. After that I went to check out the balcony and was relieved to see there was a new railing in place of the old one. That didn't mean I'd be leaning up against it any time soon. My nights of going out there to gaze at the stars were over!

I wanted to give my makeup a quick touch-up

before I met Simone and Kristine, so I headed into the bathroom.

And found a message waiting for me.

Scrawled in red lipstick on the mirror over the sink was one word: *TEASE.*

Chapter 9

I stared at the mirror in shock.

My stomach knotted in fear as I began walking backward out of the bathroom.

I didn't want to look at the bloodred message, but I couldn't tear my eyes away.

It was written in huge, jagged letters, as if the person who'd ruined a tube of MAC red to create it had been filled with rage.

The killer in *Killing Spree* had left a similar note before striking one of her victims. But that wasn't the only place I recalled seeing that shade of MAC red. Tabitha had been wearing it too.

Would she have left me a threatening message because of a stupid dress?

Or could someone have taken Tabitha's lipstick . . .

Finn!

I couldn't take it anymore.

I stormed out of my cabin and began searching the ship. It didn't take me very long to find Finn and Tabitha. They were at the Roasted Bean, feeding each other from a single chocolate cupcake. I wanted to smash that cupcake all over Finn's face—but why ruin a helpless dessert? So I walked up and slammed my hand down on their table, hard enough to make the paper cups holding their lattes shake and spill over a bit.

"I found your surprise," I told Finn.

"What are you talking about?" he asked, not even looking at me as he reached for some napkins and began mopping up the tabletop.

"The message. The one you left on my bathroom mirror." I pointed at Tabitha. "It was written in *her* lipstick."

"I don't know what you're talking about," Finn said.

"What did it say?" Tabitha asked.

"You know what it said. Both of you know."

"No, I don't," Finn insisted.

Tabitha took a sip of her latte. "Neither do I."

"It said *TEASE*. Just like in the movie we saw today."

Tabitha laughed out loud.

"What's so funny?" I demanded.

"Sounds like someone struck a nerve." She snickered. "From what I hear, that word fits you perfectly."

"I didn't write any messages on your bathroom mirror," Finn said. "Did you stop to think that maybe your new boyfriend did? He was at the movie too."

"Why would Logan do something like that?"

Finn gave me a look. "He didn't seem too happy when he left you outside the movie theater. He wanted you to go back to his cabin with him and you didn't want to."

I was outraged. "Were you eavesdropping on our conversation?"

"He works for the cruise line," Tabitha added. "With his access to card keys, he's probably able to come and go as he pleases. How would we have gotten into your cabin, Nancy Drew?"

I hated to admit it, but they had a point. Logan probably could have gotten into my cabin.

I thought he'd just been disappointed when I didn't go back to his cabin after the movie. But maybe he'd been angry.

No!

I had to trust my instincts, and I wasn't getting a bad vibe from him.

Not like I did from Finn or . . . Sam!

He had also been at the movie!

Why hadn't I realized it sooner?

Sam could have taken Charlotte's card key and left the message.

"What are you doing with these two?" Simone asked as she and Kristine came to my side.

"Nothing," I said flatly. "Let's go get a latte." I didn't want to waste any more time with Finn and Tabitha. If anything, they were only confusing me. All I knew was that if Finn *had* left me that message, he was going to regret it.

"Just stay away from me," I told Finn. "I mean it."

"Why don't you leave *him* alone?" Tabitha

asked, defending him. "You're the one who keeps coming back to him."

I left without answering. After Simone, Kristine, and I got our own table, I told them about the message and how I thought Sam might have left it. I didn't tell them that Finn had accused Logan leaving it. It would only freak Kristine out and make her suspicious of him again.

"I don't think it was Sam," Simone said. "I know you think he's weird, but you can't hold it against the guy. He can't help it. Besides, why would he do it? What's his reason? But Finn or Tabitha? They *both* had a reason and could have easily gotten into your room."

"How?"

"Easy," Simone said, taking a sip of her latte. "All they had to do was wait for the cleaning woman to go inside and then hide in a closet. Once she's gone, they get out of the closet, leave the message, and then walk out of your cabin."

"It does make sense," Kristine said.

I had to admit, it did.

"Here's another thought," Simone said. "What if the message *wasn't* for you?"

"Huh?" I asked.

"What if the message was for *Charlotte*?" Simone suggested. "It's her cabin too."

I hadn't thought of that.

But it made no sense!

Who would have left her the message? The only person I could think of was Sam. But why would he do it? Things seemed fine between them, but maybe they were having problems that I didn't know about. Sam could have lashed out by leaving the message.

I'd discuss it with Charlotte, but my gut told me that the message had been left for me.

I looked across the café to where Finn and Tabitha were sitting together. They were laughing and smiling again.

Finn turned his head and caught me staring.

He gave me a smile.

But it wasn't a nice smile.

It looked dark.

Dangerous.

And deadly.

Chapter 10

*W*hen I got back to the cabin, I found Charlotte getting dressed for dinner. As usual, she looked sophisticated and elegant. Tonight she was wearing a white silk dress with a ruffled hemline. It had a very 1920s feel to it. I knew that Charlotte loved vintage clothing and wondered if it was an original. I get the whole vintage thing, but I'm not into buying clothes that were once worn by other people.

"Where've you been?" she asked, fastening a pair of crystal chandelier earrings. They were long and dangling and went great with her dress.

"Hanging out with Simone and Kristine." That was true. But after leaving the coffee bar, I'd gone to the ship's Internet café—where I'd Googled Taylor Morton. A bunch of websites connected to newspapers, magazines, and TV stations came up. After a while they all blended together. The articles hadn't taught me anything I hadn't already known.

There were tons of photos of Taylor online too. But just staring at her face wasn't going to help me figure her out. Who was this girl? Was she an innocent victim? Or had she brought her disappearance on herself in some way?

All I knew was that she had broken Logan's heart.

Some of the articles mentioned Logan—never as a suspect—but as one of the last few people who'd seen her alive.

"I found the message you left for me on the bathroom mirror," Charlotte said. "Ha. Ha. Very funny. Just like in the movie we saw this afternoon." She spritzed some perfume on herself. The scent wafted over to me; it was light and citrusy.

"I didn't leave that message," I said.

Charlotte stopped laughing. "What do you mean you didn't leave it?"

"I found it when I came back to the cabin after the fashion show." I handed her a shopping bag that was next to our closet. "I brought you something. Why don't you see what it is?" I didn't want to freak Charlotte out. I was hoping to lighten the mood, but it wasn't working.

Charlotte ignored the shopping bag. She turned pale and almost dropped the bottle of perfume she was holding. "You mean a stranger was in our cabin?" She ran for the phone on the nightstand between our beds and picked up the receiver, getting ready to dial. "We have to call the ship's security."

"Don't!" I shouted.

"Why not?" she asked, still clutching the receiver.

"I think I know who left the message."

"You do?" She hung up the phone. *"Who?"*

"It could have been Finn."

Charlotte's body sagged with relief and she rolled her eyes. "That idiot! Only a jock would pull a stunt like that! You should have made him clean up his mess. It took me forever to get that lipstick off the mirror."

"Or it could have been someone else," I added.

"Someone else? Who?"

I didn't want to say his name. I was afraid of Charlotte's reaction. He was her *boyfriend*, after all!

"Ashley, tell me," she insisted. "Who else?"

"Sam," I whispered.

Charlotte looked at me blankly. "Sam?" Then realization washed over her face. "You've got to be kidding me! *My* Sam? You're saying my Sam did it?" Anger colored her voice. "Why would you even accuse him of something like that? Especially after he rescued you this morning!"

"He told you?"

"Yes! Why wouldn't he? He was worried about you. Now answer me, Ashley! Why are you accusing Sam?"

I didn't know what to say. I couldn't tell Charlotte that I felt like Sam was always watching me and it weirded me out.

"I don't like him," I admitted. I tried to do some damage control. "I think you could do so much better than him."

"And that's why you're saying he did it?"

"I didn't say he did it. I said he could have." Although why would he have done it? To scare me so I'd turn to him for protection? So he could act like a hero the way he had this morning when he rescued me from the sauna? "He could have borrowed your card key and left the message."

"Why?" Charlotte demanded. "Why would he do it?"

"I don't know!" I scrambled for a reason, any reason. "Maybe he was playing a joke on us. For all I know, the message was for you. We're both sharing the cabin. Did you guys have a fight?"

"Sam would never do anything like that. You shouldn't make accusations that you can't back up! I'm sorry that you don't like him, but there have been plenty of guys that you went out with that I thought were losers and I didn't say anything because you're my sister and I didn't want to hurt your feelings."

What?!

This was news to me!

"Like who?" The question slipped out before I could stop it.

"Where should I start?" Charlotte began counting off on her fingers. "How about Lenny, the drummer you dated last fall? He gave new meaning to the word *dumb*! Or Rex, the soccer player? He spent more time looking in the mirror than he did looking at you! Then there were Ken, Jason, and Rick. Do you want me to go on?"

I was stunned. Stunned! I'd had no idea Charlotte didn't like the guys I dated.

"No," I said.

"I kept my opinion to myself because who you go out with is none of my business. Just like who *I* go out with is none of yours! I don't ever want to hear you say another word against Sam, do you understand? Not another word!"

I had never seen this side of Charlotte before. Usually she was so quiet, so demure. But now she was like a raging pit bull! This was the first time we'd gotten into any sort of sisterly squabble. Until today, we'd never fought. Seeing this other side of Charlotte made her seem more human. Less than perfect.

"I'm sorry," I said, meaning it. The last thing I had wanted to do was make her upset.

She sat on her bed, rubbing the sides of her head. "Now I have a headache on top of still feeling seasick," she muttered. She stood up and walked over to the dresser and found two bottles of pills. After pouring a glass of water from a pitcher, she shook out two pills from each bottle into her hand. I recognized one Bishop Pharmaceutical bottle. There were always samples of different medications in our house.

"Is it safe to mix those?" I asked. Ever since we'd gotten on board, it seemed like Charlotte was constantly taking pills for various ailments, although she always looked perfectly healthy to me. Sometimes I wondered if she was a hypochondriac.

"Yes!" she snapped, tossing the pills into her mouth and taking a sip of water.

I'd never seen Charlotte so touchy before.

After finishing the glass of water, she walked over to her bed and began emptying a shopping bag. It looked like she had done some shopping today too.

"Want to see what I bought?" I asked, unwrapping my purchases, trying to lighten the mood.

"No," she said without even looking at me as she opened a box and took out a pair of high-heeled shoes. They were tan suede peep-toe pumps with an extremely high heel. They were gorgeous! I couldn't take my eyes off them as she brought them over to her closet. She put them away and then picked up her purse, which was a gold python print clutch, and headed for the door.

"I'm going to the dining room," she said.

"Save a place for me at your table?"

"Why?" she snapped. "I'm having dinner with Sam. You don't like him, remember?"

"I said I was sorry."

"Saying you're sorry isn't good enough. I don't want to be anywhere near you tonight, Ashley. I'm still too mad!"

And then she left.

I wanted to run after her, but I figured I'd give her some time to cool off. Hopefully, she wouldn't tell Sam what I had told her. *That* would be awkward.

After Charlotte left, I changed my clothes, deciding to wear my new peach slip dress. The dress was cute, but none of the shoes I had packed seemed to go with it.

Then I remembered Charlotte's new shoes.

They would go *perfectly* with my dress.

I raced over to the closet and pulled them out, slipping my feet into them. I was so lucky we wore the same shoe size.

This wasn't the first time I'd borrowed something of Charlotte's. Every so often I'd pop into her bedroom and borrow a sweater or top. Usually I'd ask first, though. And she hadn't had a chance to wear her new shoes yet. That should have made them off-limits to me. But I'm sure if I had asked if I could, she would have said yes.

Even though we had fought earlier, I was sure she wouldn't mind that I was borrowing the shoes. After all, that's what sisters were for, right?

The heels were wobbly. Very wobbly. Usually I didn't have a problem walking in high heels, but these were tricky. Maybe it was because the heels were so thin. I was used to wearing heels that were a bit thicker—and not as high!

Walking to the dining room—my friends and I had decided to eat in the Santorini again—took me a while, but eventually I got there. By the time I arrived, my walk was smoother.

I stood at the top of the curving staircase, staring down at everyone as they ate. I felt like a star in a movie making her big entrance. I could smell all the delicious food coming out of the kitchen and I realized how hungry I was. I began hurrying down the stairs.

It was after I took my third step that disaster struck.

I was stepping onto the fourth step when I heard a snap and then the heel on my right shoe cracked.

As soon as it did, I started to lose my balance. Then I pitched forward, my arms flailing out while my legs folded under me.

I began to fall headfirst down the staircase and my arms tried to grab something.

Anything!

If I didn't do something fast, I was going to fall all the way to the bottom!

I reached out wildly, grabbing the banister. As soon as my fingers felt the smooth wood railing, they locked around it and I stopped moving.

My body shuddered in relief and slid down onto the stairs, trying to regain control of myself. I looked down and saw how far the stairs went.

If I had fallen all the way to the bottom . . .

I didn't even want to think about it!

Anything could have happened.

I could have broken a leg.

I could have snapped my neck and become paralyzed.

Or worse.

I could have died.

I shuddered at that thought.

Why had I been in such a hurry? I knew from last night that the steps were steep. Why hadn't I gone slower?

But then I remembered something else.

My shoe.

The heel had snapped off.

I took off my right shoe and examined the broken heel.

I blinked in disbelief.

Was I seeing what I thought I was?

I brought the shoe closer to my eyes.

It looked like the heel had been sawed off and reapplied with glue.

Had Charlotte's shoe been tampered with?

But when?

And why?

"Ashley!" Charlotte ran up the stairs. "I saw what almost happened." Racing behind her were Kristine and Simone. "You scared me to death!"

"Us too!" Kristine cried.

"We thought you were going to fall all the way to the bottom," Simone said.

I held out the broken shoe to all of them. "Look!"

"Why were you wearing my shoes?" Charlotte asked, her voice thick with confusion.

"I know I shouldn't have borrowed them without asking, but they went perfectly with my dress. I couldn't resist."

Charlotte shook her head. "That's not what I meant," she explained. "You shouldn't have been wearing them because they were damaged. The clerk told me the right heel was broken and gave me a discount. That's why I bought them. I was going to have the heel repaired when we got home. They were the last pair in my size and I had to have them."

The shoe *hadn't* been tampered with!

I laughed. "The one time I borrow something of yours without asking, I almost break a leg."

"Or worse," Kristine added.

Charlotte gave me a hug. "I'm sorry I was so mad at you. If anything had happened to you, I would never have forgiven myself. I don't know what I'd do without you."

I hugged Charlotte back, glad that our first real fight was over.

"Let's go eat," I said, getting back on my feet and taking off my other shoe. "Then after dinner I'll go get a new pair of shoes and we'll party for the rest of the night!"

Chapter 11

Charlotte asked me to have dinner with her and Sam, but I told her they deserved to have a romantic evening together. Even though we had made up, I knew she was still feeling bad about what I'd said. It was written all over her face. I told her I was fine and insisted that she have a good time with Sam. She finally left me and I went to sit with Simone and Kristine.

As we walked across the dining room, I could see Finn and Tabitha sitting together in a corner. They were holding hands and I could see Tabitha rubbing Finn's leg under the table with her foot. For once, Finn wasn't looking in my direction.

"Girl, you sure do love your drama," Simone said as we sat down.

"You nearly scared me to death," Kristine added.

"I scared myself too," I said. "But it's over and done with." I turned to Simone. "So, how goes the guy hunting?"

"It doesn't," Simone grumbled, chomping on a breadstick. "I struck out again today."

"Poor Simone," Kristine teased. "She's having a dry spell."

"We can't all be as lucky as Ashley." Simone looked around the dining room. "So, where is Mr. Adorable?"

Good question. I tried to find Logan among the waiters, but I didn't see him. When Molly came to our table with menus, I asked if she knew where he was.

"Tonight he's working in the dining room on the Diablo Deck," she said. "But he asked me to give you a message. He said he'll meet you at Club Paradise around nine. And he promises to be there on time tonight."

Molly's message from Logan thrilled me. It meant he wasn't mad at me for not going back to his cabin with him.

We decided on seafood for dinner and ordered shrimp cocktails as appetizers and lobsters for our main course. We wore big plastic bibs around our necks as we cracked open the lobsters and searched for the sweet tender meat inside. They were messy to eat, but sooo good! For dessert, we went with chocolate soufflés that gave new meaning to the phrase *sinfully delicious*.

Once dinner was over we headed back to my cabin so I could get a new pair of shoes and then we went off to Club Paradise. When I got there, I found a nice surprise: Logan!

He was wearing loafers, khakis, a plum-colored polo shirt, and a tan sport jacket, looking all nice and summery, like he'd stepped out of the pages of a J. Crew catalog.

"You beat me here!" I said.

"I wanted to make up for last night," he said, pulling me into his arms and giving me a kiss. It was just as hot and heavy as the one he'd given me that afternoon.

"I missed you," he said.

"I missed you too," I said as I kissed him back, savoring the feel of his lips against mine.

"Aren't you going to introduce us?" Simone asked from behind me.

Reluctantly, I broke my kiss with Logan and turned around, pointing to Simone and Kristine. "These are my two best friends," I said, "although if they interrupt me the next time I'm kissing you, I'm going to hurt them."

"She must like you," Simone said. "She only threatens bodily harm when she likes a guy."

Logan nodded hello. Soon the music started and we headed out to the dance floor.

We danced for two hours nonstop. The d.j. played everything from classic disco, hip-hop, rap, and current hits. There was no stopping Logan. And there was no stopping me! I hadn't had this much fun dancing in a long time. Whenever a new song started, I lost myself in the music, letting my body sway to the rhythm and lyrics. Finn had never liked dancing, and the few times that we had gone, we'd hardly stayed. Tonight I was making up for lost time!

After another song ended, Logan walked to our table, where we'd ordered some sodas, and took a sip. Then he wiped his forehead with a napkin. We were both working up a bit of a sweat. We definitely needed to take a break.

"I need some fresh air to cool off," he said.

"Why don't we go out on the deck?" I suggested. It would be nice to be by ourselves for a while. Even though Kristine and Simone were giving us our space, they were still around. I didn't feel like Logan and I had had any alone time this evening and I wanted that.

We left Club Paradise and headed out to the deck. It had stopped raining a few hours earlier and the temperature had dropped. Having come from inside a hot dance club, I could immediately feel the chill in the air and I shivered.

"Here," Logan said, taking off his sport jacket and wrapping it around my shoulders. "This will keep you warm."

"Thanks," I said, pulling it close around me. I buried my nose in its collar, inhaling Logan's scent as I leaned against a railing. "How long have you been working on this ship?"

"Two years. I start when school ends and then I work all the way through Labor Day. Then I go back home."

"Where's home?"

"Brooklyn."

"Really?" I exclaimed, all excited. "I live in Manhattan! We're practically neighbors."

"That means we can see each other when we get back," he said. "That is, if you still want to."

"Give me a reason for wanting to see you," I said coyly.

"How about this?" he asked as he leaned in and kissed me again.

It was the perfect setting for a romantic kiss. There was a full moon in the sky, the stars were twinkling, and Logan was holding me close.

When the kiss ended, I asked Logan, "Are you going to be a senior this year?"

"Yep."

"Do you know where you want to go to college?"

"I haven't made up my mind yet but I'd like to go away. Maybe UCLA or USC."

That was all the way across the country! If Logan and I started dating, I would never see him after his senior year.

Wait, wait, wait! *Slow down, Ashley!* I scolded myself. I didn't even know if we'd still be seeing each other after this cruise. But I wanted to. Very much.

"My sister, Charlotte, is going to be a senior this year. She's been studying like crazy. She doesn't go anywhere without her SAT prep book."

"Where does she want to go?"

"Princeton, Harvard, Yale. She'll get into all of them. She's that smart. My dad's thrilled. He's finally going to have an Ivy League graduate."

"Did he actually say that?"

"Not exactly," I said, realizing how it sounded. "My dad's not like that. He's *never* compared me to Charlotte and he would never say anything that would hurt either one of us. It's just that I know how important being number one is to him. I mean, he *is* a workaholic. That's why his company is so successful. Even if he won't say he wants me to be number one, it's easy to figure out."

"How?"

"There's always a smile on his face when he looks at Charlotte's report card or hears of her latest accomplishment. When he looks at my report card, he'll compliment me on my good grades, but then ask that I try harder in my other classes where my grades aren't as high because he knows I'm capable of more. It's always been that way, even before Charlotte came to live with us, but I guess I'm just more aware of it now."

"Does that bother you? Being compared to Charlotte?"

I thought about Logan's question. "If I wanted, I suppose I could be resentful, but I've never felt any anger or jealousy toward Charlotte. I've never felt that Daddy loves her more than me. I know that he loves us the same and he wants the best for both of us."

"Well, when the day comes that you do finally graduate, where do you want to go to college?"

"I'll go to whatever college will take me," I joked.

"Maybe you need a little one-on-one tutoring to pull up your grades."

"Have anyone in mind?"

Logan cupped my face in his hands, staring deep into my eyes. I stared back into his and I could see there was a moment of hesitation. What was he searching for? What did he see?

"I'd love to spend some time alone with you," he said before pressing his lips to mine and opening my mouth with his. It was a deep kiss, one that I felt throughout my entire body. It set me on fire and made me want more, much more.

"I bet you would," I gasped, breaking the kiss and wiggling out of his arms. Things were starting to pick up speed again. There was this chemistry between us. It was fun and it was electrifying but I wanted more than just a physical thing between us.

"What do you want to do when you graduate from college?" I asked, starting to walk along the deck, taking Logan's hand in mine. "Have you thought that far ahead? Are you thinking of becoming a photographer?"

"How'd you guess?"

"Those pictures gave me a clue."

"I'd love to pursue my photography. Maybe become a photojournalist and travel around the world."

I noticed there was a passion and excitement in Logan's voice when he talked about his photography.

"But it's a tough field to break into," he said. "And it doesn't pay a lot. At least not at first."

"You could always join the paparazzi," I teased. "You know, chase after famous celebrities."

Logan made a face. "Those guys are vultures. How would you like it if someone was always sticking a camera in your face or hiding in the bushes outside your house, waiting to jump out at you with a camera?"

"I wouldn't," I admitted.

"How about you?" he asked. "What do you want to do someday? If the stylist thing doesn't work out, do you have a backup plan?"

"I don't even know what college I want to get into!" I exclaimed. "I need to figure that out first. Sometimes I wish I was more focused, like Charlotte."

"Your sister seems nice."

"She is. But I still don't feel like I really know her."

"You have a lot of lost years to make up for. Be patient. It'll happen."

"I know."

"So, your future."

"In case you haven't figured it out yet, I *love* clothes. Being a stylist is high on my list, but I'd also love to work in fashion. Maybe as a buyer for a department store. They get to go to all those runway shows in Europe, and they meet with the designers in their showrooms. Or maybe become a journalist and write about clothes for a big magazine like *Elle* or *Vogue*."

"Did you know your face lights up when you talk about fashion?"

I blushed. "It does?"

Logan nodded. "Don't be embarrassed. You really have a passion for it. That counts for a lot. If you want it badly enough, it'll happen."

"I'll call you ten years from now and let you know."

"Deal!" Logan exclaimed. "Who knows? Maybe I'll be photographing the clothes that you'll be writing about."

"Besides taking pictures, what do you do for fun when you're at home?" I asked.

"I usually hang out with my friends. Go to movies, play video games. I'm into soccer and basketball. And I go to a lot of concerts."

"Who are your favorite bands?"

"Green Day. Maroon Five. The Black Eyed Peas. How about you?"

How did I tell Logan that I was *the* party girl of my high school? That I lived for shopping? That I loved throwing parties and was addicted to reality TV? Or that when it came to concerts I usually went for female solo artists like Christina Aguilera, Beyoncé, Rihanna, Pink, or Gwen Stefani?

On the surface, it didn't seem like we had a lot in common, but we seemed to click. And don't they say that opposites usually attract?

"Do you have a girlfriend back home?"

Where had that question come from?! Was my mouth working independently of my brain?

Logan dropped my hand and gave me a stunned look. I could see I had hurt him with my question.

"If I had a girlfriend, would I be here with you?" he asked. "What kind of guy do you think I am?"

"Logan, I'm sorry." My words came out in a rush. "I didn't mean anything. The question just popped out."

Obviously, I'd hit a sore spot and it made

me think of Taylor Morton again. From what Molly had told me, Taylor had been cheating on Logan with another guy. Having gone through the pain of that, I'm sure Logan would never do that to someone else. He was obviously still carrying the scars of his relationship with her.

How could she have treated him so horribly? He was a great guy.

"Logan, I know you would never cheat on a girl. I don't know where the question came from. Well, actually, I do," I admitted. "Not all the guys I've gone out with in the past have been as nice as you. And I've dated a two-timer. It was force of habit."

"Sounds like this guy really hurt you. Who was it? Finn?"

I shook my head. "No, not Finn. His name was Rick. We dated last year. Over the summer he went to work at a sleepaway camp as a counselor. At first we were constantly talking on the phone and e-mailing, but as the summer went on, I started hearing from him less and less. I didn't want to be one of those pesky girlfriends, always hounding her boyfriend with questions like, 'Where are you?' 'What are you doing?'

'Why aren't I hearing from you?' I trusted him and assumed he was really busy."

"But he wasn't?"

"Oh, he was busy—*getting* busy with another girl," I explained. "He called me the day before he was due back home to tell me over the phone. I felt like an idiot for not figuring it out sooner."

"You couldn't have known," Logan said. "You trusted the guy."

"And then Finn was such a jerk." I stared into Logan's eyes, hoping he could see how much I meant the words I was about to say. "I guess I'm finding it hard to believe that I've finally found a really nice guy. I feel like I'm dreaming."

"Want me to pinch you so you can see you're not?"

"No!"

"But then I'd kiss you and make it all better."

I bet he would too.

I reached for Logan's hand, waiting to see if he would let me hold it. "Still friends?"

"Still friends," he said, clasping his hand

around mine and leading me back to the deck's railing so we could gaze at the stars. He stopped behind me, wrapping his arms around my waist, pushing me against the railing as he leaned into me.

I instantly felt uncomfortable.

But not because of Logan.

Being pressed so close against the railing made me think of what had almost happened the night before.

It also made me think of Taylor.

Had she been standing in a spot similar to this a year ago?

Had someone come up and pushed her overboard?

Could she have jumped?

Or had she slipped?

I pushed myself away from the railing and into Logan, who stumbled a few inches back.

"Hey, what's wrong?" he asked, his voice sounding startled.

"Nothing." I turned around with a smile and gave him a quick kiss. "Are you ready to dance some more?"

"Ready if you are."

"Then let's go!"

As we walked back inside, I looked over my shoulder at the sea one last time, wondering if I was looking at Taylor Morton's grave.

We danced for another two hours until finally I was exhausted. My feet couldn't take it anymore. Even though they looked fab in the shoes I'd changed into, they were *aching*. Simone and Kristine had already left the club so it was just Logan and me.

We left Club Paradise together and headed for the elevator. As we walked, I wondered if Logan was going to ask me to come back to his cabin. If he did, I didn't know what I was going to say. I've always felt that when it came to my first time, I would *know*. Instinctively.

I still wasn't sure. The truth was, I barely knew Logan.

But maybe it was like swimming for the first time. You just had to take the plunge.

"What floor are you on?" Logan asked as we walked into the elevator and the doors closed behind us.

"Six."

He pressed the button for six and then two, which was his floor. The elevator started to descend.

"Have you ever done this before?" he asked, pressing the stop button. The elevator instantly came to a halt. Then he turned to me with a devilish grin and began walking closer, backing me into a corner of the elevator. My heart began pounding with excitement as I wondered what was going to happen next.

Once I was in the corner, he reached for my arms, holding them over my head with one hand.

Then he started kissing me.

First he started along the side of my neck, leaving a trail of kisses. One. Two. Three. Then he arrived at my face, kissing my cheeks before moving to my lips.

His kisses were intoxicating—I felt like an addict who wanted more, more, more!

I wanted to wrap my arms around him, but I couldn't, so instead I wrapped a leg around him, pulling him close as his free hand began moving up my other leg and along my back. With Logan's every kiss and touch, my entire body was crackling with tingles of excitement.

Just as I started to wonder how far we would go, we heard voices.

"Is there something wrong with this elevator?"

"Why isn't it coming? I keep pressing the button."

Logan pulled away from me. "Looks like the party's over," he said, hitting the start button. The elevator began moving. Seconds later it stopped on six. My legs felt like jelly, but I managed to walk off the elevator.

"See you tomorrow," I said, wanting him to step off the elevator and follow me back to my cabin. I wanted to say the words, but I couldn't get them out. Part of me did, but another part wanted Logan to take control and make the decision for me.

He didn't.

"Sweet dreams," he said as the elevator doors closed on him, giving me that same devilish smile he had earlier.

Once I got back to my cabin, I changed into an oversized T-shirt, washed my face, brushed my teeth, and collapsed into bed. Charlotte still wasn't back, but I figured I'd hear her when she came in.

I didn't.

I fell asleep as soon as my head hit the pillow.

The next time I woke up, the phone was ringing.

At first I was disoriented, not knowing where I was. Then my eyes focused on the digital clock by the side of the bed. It was three A.M.

I stumbled in the dark, hurrying to answer the phone so it wouldn't wake up Charlotte.

"Hello?" I said, my voice groggy and heavy with sleep.

At the other end of the line, I could hear heavy breathing.

"Hello?" I said again, waiting for someone to say something. "Is anyone there?"

There was still no answer.

Just the sound of breathing.

As sleep faded away, I suddenly thought of the movie I had seen the previous day and my blood turned cold.

The killer had called some of her victims before striking. She hadn't said anything. All she had done was breathe.

I hung up the phone.

Then I turned on the light on the nightstand, wanting to talk to Charlotte.

I hated to admit it, but the phone call had scared me.

But when the light filled the cabin, Charlotte's bed was empty.

At first I panicked. *Where was she?* But then I quickly calmed down. She was either still out partying or she was spending the night with Sam.

Were *Charlotte and Sam* sleeping together? Charlotte and I never discussed personal stuff like that. She never asked me anything about the guys I dated, and I had never asked her anything about Sam. She was always so private. I knew everything about Simone's and Kristine's love lives—Simone had already done it; Kristine hadn't—but nothing about my older half sister's. I didn't even know if Sam was the first guy she'd dated. She hadn't told me much about her old life in San Francisco. I guess I had always assumed that Charlotte would be the kind of girl who would wait until she got married—it was just a vibe that she gave off. Always being so perfect and never breaking the rules—but what did I really know about her? Not much.

Sometimes I felt like we were strangers. In a way, I guess we were. We had so many years to make up for. We'd hardly scratched the surface of getting to know each other. When Charlotte first moved in, I had bombarded her with questions. She'd answered them, but I could tell it still hurt talking about everything she'd left behind in San Francisco. So I stopped asking questions, figuring Charlotte would talk when she was ready. After two years, I was still waiting for her to talk.

The phone rang again, startling me.

I stared at it, hoping it would stop ringing.

But it didn't.

It just rang.

And rang.

And rang.

Finally, I couldn't take it anymore, and

I snatched it up, not saying anything. I just listened.

And waited.

Waited to hear some sort of sound from the other end.

Because I knew something was going to happen. It was a feeling deep in my bones.

A bad feeling.

And then I heard it again.

The sound of heavy breathing.

Chapter 12

The breathing went on and on and on.

I couldn't stand hearing it. It cut through me like a knife.

Who was on the other end of the line? Why were they doing this to me?

I didn't know what do do.

I felt paralyzed with fear.

I wanted to do *something*. Anything!

But before I could find my voice, the line went dead.

After I hung up the phone, I called Simone and Kristine. I couldn't deal with this by myself.

As I waited for them to arrive, the walls of the cabin began to feel like they were closing in on me. I tried walking around, but it didn't help. The feeling kept getting worse and worse. I felt like I was going to be crushed at any second. Was this what people who suffered from claustrophobia went through?

I tried to take a deep breath, but I couldn't. Suddenly, I couldn't breathe. My throat felt like it was closing.

I headed to the sliding glass door that led out to the balcony and opened it, letting in a cool night breeze. I inhaled deeply as the air washed over me, seeping through the thin nightshirt I was wearing, my panic subsiding. I shivered, but it wasn't because I was cold.

I was thinking of the heavy breathing.

What had happened when the line went dead?

Before I could dwell on my thoughts any longer, there was a knock on the cabin door. I left the sliding glass door and cautiously approached it.

"Who is it?" I asked.

"Us!" Simone exclaimed.

"Open the door!" Kristine whispered, knowing that most of the ship was asleep. "Let us in!"

I quickly unlocked the door and they hurried

inside. Both were wearing oversized robes over their pajamas, and Kristine's face was shiny with the moisturizer she slathered over her face every night before she went to sleep.

"What's wrong?" Simone asked.

"What happened?" Kristine asked. "You sounded petrified."

"And you *look* petrified," Simone said, staring at me, "and not because your hair is a mess and you've got sleep wrinkles all over your face. What's going on?"

I hadn't said anything when I'd called and woken them up. I'd just begged them to come to my cabin.

I told them about the phone call.

"You're not *really* freaking out over a phone call, are you?" Simone asked, plumping up my pillows and leaning against the headboard of my bed, making herself comfortable. She gave me a smirk—which I found *extremely* irritating. Like she knew something I didn't. She looked at me like I was crazy.

"Then what was going on?" I asked, trying not to sound defensive.

"A practical joke!" Simone exclaimed.

"A practical joke?" I whispered as her words sank in. My fear instantly disappeared, replaced by anger. "You mean to tell me the two of you—"

She cut me off. "No! Not us! Come on, Ashley! Would we really play such a horrible joke on you?"

"Why would we even do such a thing?" Kristine added.

"Then who?" I demanded. "Who?"

"Who do you think?" Kristine asked.

My brain was on overload. Too much was going on and it was hard for me to sort through it all. I felt like such a fool! How could I let one phone call freak me out?

Simone jumped off my bed. "Think, Ashley! Who are the two people on this cruise out to make sure you don't have a good time?"

It didn't take very long for two names to pop into my head.

"Finn and Tabitha," I said, feeling defeated.

Simone nodded. "That's right. I bet they cooked up this little prank just to scare you."

"Well, it worked!"

"It works only if you let them know they scared you," Simone added. "I'm sure they're going to expect you to accuse them of it. Don't even mention it to them. That'll drive them crazy!"

"She's right," Kristine said.

I'm *totally* opposed to violence of any sort, but at that moment I wanted to scratch Tabitha's eyes out. That witch! Talk about a twisted sense of humor.

And Finn. I could see him trying not to burst into laughter while Tabitha was breathing into the phone. Since he knew how paranoid I get after seeing a horror movie, I'm sure he had enjoyed every second of scaring me. The whole thing had probably been his idea!

"I won't say anything," I agreed, silently vowing that I was going to find some way to get even with Finn and Tabitha.

Kristine yawned. "I guess we should be getting back to our cabin."

Even though the mystery of the phone call had been solved, I didn't want to be alone.

"Do you guys mind spending the rest of the

night with me? Please? I'm still feeling a little jittery."

"Hey," Simone said, glancing around the cabin and then staring at Charlotte's perfectly made bed. "Where's Miss Charlotte?"

Miss Charlotte was Simone's nickname for my sister. I don't want to say they didn't get along, but whenever they were together there was a distinct chill in the air. Simone had told me more than once that she thought Charlotte needed to loosen up and have some fun. Charlotte, although she had never said anything negative about Simone, made it clear through passing comments to me that she thought Simone focused too much on guys and partying and should be directing that same amount of attention on her classes. I couldn't exactly disagree. Simone's grades had taken a bit of a dip last semester, but I knew she was going to buckle down once classes started again. Junior and senior year were too important not to.

I shrugged. "I guess she's with Sam."

Simone gasped faux dramatically. "You mean Char is getting some?"

"I don't know," I said, not wanting to discuss

it. "She didn't tell me." I pointed a warning finger at Simone. "And if you see her tomorrow, don't ask!"

Simone pulled down the sheets of Charlotte's bed, slipping underneath them. "Well, if she comes back while I'm still here, she's fair game!"

"Simone!"

Simone had stayed out all night this spring for the first time when we were spending the weekend at her house in the Hamptons. It was when she met her last boyfriend, Joey.

"Okay! Okay! I won't razz her! But it's nice to know that she's not always studying."

"Where am I supposed to sleep?" Kristine asked, staring pointedly at Simone, who was hogging the entire bed and wouldn't budge an inch.

"Sorry, but when it comes to my beauty sleep, I don't do sharing," Simone said, stretching out her body and wrapping herself tightly in the sheets.

"You can sleep in my bed," I told Kristine, slipping under the sheets and scootching over.

"It's big enough for two."

We all talked for a little bit in the dark, but then Simone and Kristine drifted off to sleep.

I didn't.

I was still uneasy. It was like I was expecting something else to happen. How many scary things can happen before you have to admit it's more than just coincidence? At least I wasn't alone, I thought. Thank God for Kristine and Simone.

The next morning we arrived in the Bahamas. Our ship was pulling into Nassau when we woke up, and I couldn't wait to start exploring the island.

"If any guys see us on the way back to our cabin, you're going to owe us big time," Simone vowed as they left my cabin at around nine, checking to make sure the coast was clear. Simone rarely left her room unless she was perfectly done-up. She was currently rocking the bed-head, no makeup look. Not that she looked bad, but try telling her that.

"We'll see you at breakfast," Kristine said.

"Let's go to the English Muffin on the Panama Deck. They're supposed to serve scones and clotted cream like they do in London. Thirty minutes?"

"They also serve kippers," Simone said.

"Kippers? What are those?"

"I think they're either herring or fried sardines."

Kristine made a face. "Ick! I'll pass on those!"

"I think I might try them," Simone said as Kristine turned green at the thought. I laughed, knowing Simone had only said that to get a reaction out of Kristine.

"See you in a little bit," I said, closing my cabin door.

After they left, I hopped into the shower. When I came out of the bathroom, toweling my hair dry, I was startled to see Charlotte standing at the dresser, still wearing her clothes from the night before.

"Oh!"

"Sorry, I didn't mean to scare you." She tossed a handful of pills into her mouth and swallowed. I wondered what they were for, but didn't ask. "I came in while you were in the shower."

"That's okay," I said, running a comb through my damp hair and deciding to pull it into a ponytail. If I left it loose, the humidity would turn it into a frizzy poof.

"Where were you last night?" I asked.

"Out."

"I know that. But with who?"

Charlotte rolled her eyes. "With Sam. Who else?"

Simone, Kristine, and I always told each other every single detail of our dates. I was waiting for the same thing from Charlotte. Even though I wasn't crazy about Sam, I was dying for her to spill. I waited for her to dish, but she didn't. I asked if she had a good time and what they had done, but she only gave me short, vague answers. Finally, I gave up. If she wanted to tell me anything, she would. And if she didn't, well, there was nothing I could do about that. Although I admit it hurt. After all, I was her sister. Aren't sisters supposed to tell each other everything?

"Who slept in my bed last night?" she asked,

noticing the messed sheets.

"Kristine and Simone spent the night. We had a sleepover." I decided to change the subject because I didn't want to discuss last night. Two could play the same game. "Are you and Sam exploring the island today?"

"Not until this afternoon." She held up her SAT prep book. "I need to do some studying. I want to take a practice test and see how well I do."

Was she serious? "Charlotte! We're on vacation."

"So?" She reached into a drawer and pulled out a swimsuit and T-shirt, heading for the bathroom.

"So, can't you allow yourself a little time to kick back and relax?"

She shook her head. "I messed up on the last test I took. I need to do better."

"It was a fake test!"

"So?"

"It doesn't count!"

"What if it was the real thing?"

"But it wasn't! That's why it's called a practice test! You're *practicing* for the real thing."

Charlotte shook her head. "I have to get the best possible score so I can earn a scholarship."

"Scholarship? Are you serious?" I laughed. "Daddy can pay for any college you want to go to."

"I don't want his money," Charlotte snapped. "I don't need it."

I was taken aback by the anger in her voice. "Why not?"

"I lived without it most of my life."

"That's not true!" I snapped back, rushing to my father's defense. "Daddy always sent your mother his support checks and he *always* remembered to send you gifts. And he always, always visited you when he was in California. He never neglected you or forgot about you."

Charlotte seemed surprised by my anger and backed off on hers. "Well, I won't need his money after this year. Once I'm in college, the only person I want to rely on is myself. Dad only took me in after my mom died because he had no choice."

I gasped. "*Charlotte!* That's not true! Daddy loves you. He's always loved you."

"Has he?" she asked, her voice thick with skepticism.

"You sound like you don't believe me."

Charlotte shrugged. "For someone who loved me so much, I rarely got to see him when I was growing up."

And whose fault was that? I wanted to say. I don't know what the deal was between Charlotte's mother and our father. When I was little, I remember hearing my parents whispering about it. I got the sense that my father wanted to see more of Charlotte, but her mother wouldn't let him. I wonder if Charlotte knew that. And I wondered if maybe Charlotte's mother had poisoned her against our father. I knew that sometimes happened when couples got divorced.

"You know how hard Daddy works," I said. "Always traveling for business. I didn't get to see him as much as I wanted to, either."

"But you always had him," Charlotte pointed out.

"And now you have him too," I said. "The past is over. Focus on the future. Make up for lost time."

Once we got home, I planned to say something to Daddy. He needed to know how Charlotte felt. I knew the news was going to upset him, but I had to tell him. Maybe he needed to make an extra effort with Charlotte. Clear up ancient history and let her know how much he'd always loved and cared for her.

Charlotte sighed. "You're right. I know Dad loves me. I don't know why I said all the things I did." She shook her head. "I'm not thinking clearly."

I gave Charlotte a hug. "Don't forget—*I* love you too."

Charlotte hugged me back. "I won't."

I was finishing up breakfast with Simone and Kristine when Logan came up to our table. He was wearing a white tank top and blue swim trunks. He looked like he was ready for a day at the beach.

"Guess who has today off?" he said, the sun glinting off the mirrored lenses of his aviator sunglasses.

I pretended to think before answering, looking him up and down. "Molly?"

He laughed. "Very funny. I thought we could go into Nassau and explore the beach. Maybe do some snorkeling."

I squirmed uncomfortably in my seat and Logan instantly noticed.

"What's wrong?"

"I already made plans with Simone and Kristine," I said.

"That's okay," Simone said, giving Logan a sweet smile. "We understand."

"Totally," Kristine added.

Simone then turned and gave me that piercing look of hers, the look that meant she expected me to get alone with Logan and then come back with some sort of sexy story to share.

"We'll see you guys later," Kristine said, getting out of her seat. Simone followed after her, but not before giving me the look one last time.

"Well, I guess I'm all yours," I said to Logan. "I'd love to spend the day with you!"

Logan's entire face lit up with a smile. It was all I could do not to kiss him or run my fingers through his curly hair.

"I'll meet you at the downstairs lounge in ten minutes," he said. "That's where we have to take one of the tenders to get to the island."

"What's a tender?" I asked.

"It's a small boat. We board downstairs and it will take us to the dock. At the end of the day, it will bring us back to the ship."

"Okay, I'll be waiting."

After Logan left, Molly came over to the table to clear away the dishes. She had a worried expression on her face.

"He's falling for you," she told me.

"Is he?" I asked, taking a sip of my orange juice.

She nodded.

"Is that a bad thing?"

"I don't know," she said. "You tell me. Logan isn't the kind of guy who goes from girl to girl. He's not a player."

"I didn't think he was." It was one of the things I liked about him.

"But some of the girls on these cruises aren't looking for anything serious. They want to cut loose and have a little fun with a new guy before going back home to their boyfriends. Taylor

Morton was like that. I don't want to see Logan get hurt again. It took him all year to get over her," Molly explained. "It's not easy for him to open up to people, but you're the first girl he's gotten close to since her."

"I don't have a boyfriend back home," I told Molly.

"No, but you have an *ex*-boyfriend on board," she pointed out. "And you guys were a couple just a few days ago."

"It's over with Finn," I said. "I'm not going to hurt Logan."

"You'd better not," Molly said, almost like a warning, as she loaded her tray with dishes and glasses and lifted it to her shoulder. "Because if you do, I don't know what will happen."

After Molly left, her words remained with me. It was nice that she was looking out for Logan, but he was a big boy. He knew how to take care of himself. And I certainly wasn't going to hurt him. No relationship was perfect. They all had their ups and downs.

I was going to be myself. That's all I could be.

Chapter 13

*W*hen I met Logan to board the tender, he had a small picnic basket with him. Totally romantic!

"What's inside?" I asked, trying to lift the lid so I could get a peek.

He gave me a mysterious smile. "You'll find out later."

After waving our cabin card keys in front of a scanner that kept track of everyone who left the ship, we were allowed to board the tender. As we pulled away from our cruise ship, I couldn't help but notice how beautiful the water was. It was amazingly clear and sparkling, like a sheet of sky-blue glass.

"Look!" I pointed out to Logan as I saw rainbow-hued fish swimming by.

"You should see them up close when you're snorkeling," he said. "The colors are amazing."

We arrived at the dock in fifteen minutes and decided to explore the shopping district before going to the beach. As we walked along the stalls, we could hear the sounds of calypso music from a live band. The air was also thick with the exotic scents of roasting meats and spices. It was all so new and different, and I loved every second of it.

As we were walking, Logan slipped his hand in mine. I don't think he did it consciously. He was peeking into a stall selling straw baskets, and I was a few inches away from him. I think he reached for my hand because he didn't want to lose me. I didn't care what the reason was. Having his hand in mine felt right.

We went from stall to stall, holding hands, and when we reached the stall selling jewelry, we had to stop. Correction. *I* had to stop. There were so many pieces made from seashells, I couldn't make up my mind.

"How about this?" Logan asked, slipping a bracelet of tiny white and pink seashells around my wrist.

"It's gorgeous!" I exclaimed. I turned to the vendor, a pretty young woman with dreadlocks and skin the color of toffee. "How much?"

"Don't worry about the price," Logan said, reaching into his back pocket for his wallet. "Just tell me if you love it."

"You know I do," I said, holding out my wrist and admiring the bracelet.

"Then it's yours," he said, handing some folded bills to the young woman.

"If you're buying me a present, then I'm buying you one too," I insisted.

"You don't have to buy me something," Logan said, wrapping an arm around my waist and pulling me close. He whispered in my ear. "You can give me something when we're alone on the beach."

I turned my head to glance over my shoulder at him. "Like what?"

"A kiss?"

"I think that can be arranged," I said with a smile.

We left the shopping area and took a bus to the beach. When we finally arrived, I was stunned by the color of the sand. It was pure white. And so soft! Not at all rough and scratchy like the sand back home. Walking barefoot in it was like walking in baby powder.

We headed to the farthest end of the beach, to a spot underneath the cliffs. There weren't as many people as there were on the other parts of the beach, but that was okay. We wanted to be alone.

Once we stopped walking Logan reached into the picnic basket and took out a white sheet. I helped him open it up and spread it out on the sand. Then he sat down and took off his tank top.

"Aren't you going to sit next to me?" he asked, staring up at me.

It was the moment I had been waiting for.

Before meeting Logan for the tender, I'd gone back to my cabin and changed into a bathing suit different from the one I'd first put on. That one had been fine for a day at the beach with my girlfriends, but the one I was wearing now was made for a day at the beach with a guy you wanted to impress.

I pulled the T-shirt I was wearing over the top of my head, revealing the neon-pink bikini halter top underneath.

Then I unzipped my denim shorts and stepped

out of them, revealing a matching bikini bottom. I did a little twirl in front of Logan.

"You like?"

"I like a lot," he growled, grabbing me by the legs and pulling me down onto the sheet.

I laughed as I lost my balance and he collapsed on top of me.

His chest was pressed against mine and our faces were inches apart. His skin was warm from the sun, as smooth as leather, and I could smell the minty freshness of his breath.

"How about that kiss that you owe me?" he asked.

I placed my hands on the sides of his head and pulled him close, pressing my lips against his.

It was only supposed to be one kiss, but one wasn't enough. We kept kissing and kissing and, as we did, Logan's hands traveled from the top of my shoulders, down my arms, across my stomach, and then down my legs. My body reacted everywhere he touched me with tiny jolts of pleasure that grew more intense the longer his hands lingered. Meanwhile, my hands were doing some exploring of their own down the expanse of Logan's muscular back.

Logan broke our kiss. "How about we go swimming? It's getting kind of hot."

I wasn't sure if he was talking about us or the sun, but swimming sounded like a good idea.

"Okay," I said as I hopped to my feet and raced for the water, plunging right in.

The water wasn't cold at all. It was warm, like a bath. Logan jumped in after me and we started splashing each other. Then we started swimming, floating on our backs, staring at the sky, and pointing out the different shapes we saw in the clouds. I saw a rabbit, a horse, a tulip, and a train, while Logan saw a wolf, a duck, a donut, and a spaceship. Finally, we had enough of the water and headed back to our sheet.

"Are you hungry?" Logan asked.

"A little," I admitted.

Logan reached into the picnic basket and began pulling out all sorts of delicacies. There was a nice selection of breads, cheeses, mixed olives, a fresh bean salad, grapes, cherries, and chunks of watermelon. We dug right in.

"That hit the spot," I said, patting my lips with a napkin.

"Have any room for dessert?"

I shook my head. "I'm stuffed."

"Are you sure?"

"Why?" I can always find room for dessert. "What did you bring?"

Logan reached into the picnic basket and pulled out a can of whipped cream. I waited for him to take something else out of the basket, like a pie to squirt the whipped cream on, but he didn't.

"Where's the rest of dessert?" I asked.

"This is it," he said, showing me the can.

I was confused, but before I could ask another question, Logan shook the can and squirted a line of whipped cream around my neck. Then he began licking it off with his tongue.

The sensation was amazing! But why should Logan have all the fun?

"My turn!" I cried, taking the can out of his hand and squirting two dollops on his chest. I promptly made them disappear with my lips. Yum!

We kept passing the can of whipped cream back and forth to each other until finally it was empty.

"You were delicious," Logan said as we lay next to each other on the sheet.

"I never knew I tasted so good," I giggled. I was putting sunblock on my arms and legs and handed Logan the bottle. "Could you do my back?"

I flipped onto my stomach as Logan began applying the sunblock. Then he moved to the backs of my arms and legs. Like before, when we'd been kissing, I loved the way his hands felt all over me.

"Logan?"

"Yes?"

"Can I ask you a question?"

"Sure."

"It's personal," I said as he continued to rub in the sunblock.

"How personal?"

"Very."

He laughed. "Sounds serious."

I don't know why I was doing this, but I had to. If things were going to go farther between

Logan and me, then I wanted him to know that I cared about him, that I wasn't having a summer fling. I wanted him to put Taylor behind him so he could move forward with me. I didn't want him thinking of her when he was looking at me or wondering if I was going to break his heart the way she had.

And I wanted to know that he trusted me.

I paused. And then I just said it. "Tell me about Taylor."

He stopped rubbing in sunblock.

"How do you know about Taylor?"

At that moment, I wished I could take back my words, but they were out there. And I wanted answers.

"I saw her picture in your cabin yesterday," I said, turning around. Logan's back was to me and I could see his entire body was tense. He wasn't happy that I'd brought up Taylor's name. "Remember? And I read about her disappearance."

"What about her? What do you want to know?"

"Who was she to you?"

"A girl that I dated last summer. I had

feelings for her, but she didn't have feelings for me."

"How did you meet her?"

"On the cruise. We started talking one day. She saw me with my camera, taking some pictures, and started asking me questions. She told me she wanted to be a model, and I offered to take some pictures of her. After that, we started hanging out whenever we could. She was on the cruise for two weeks and we spent a lot of time together. We dated."

"And you fell in love with her."

Logan turned around to face me. His face was no longer warm and happy and laughing like it had been a little while ago. Now it was filled with pain—pain that I had caused by making him remember.

"Yes," he whispered. "I fell in love with her. And at first, I thought she loved me. She acted like she did. She talked about how we'd keep in touch. How we'd visit each other during the holidays and school breaks. How she was going to get a job on the ship this summer and how we'd go to the same college. But then, as the end of the cruise got closer, she changed."

"Changed?" I asked. "How?"

"She started to pull back. She didn't want to spend as much time with me. We'd make dates and she'd stand me up. Finally, she came to my cabin the night before we were supposed to arrive back in Miami and confessed everything. She told me she had a boyfriend back home. A serious boyfriend. She had been going out with him for two years. She said she loved him but that she also loved me. How can you be in love with two people at the same time?" he asked bitterly.

"You can't," I said, reaching out and gently putting a hand on his cheek. "You can only be in love with one person at one time."

I wished I could take away Logan's pain.

But I couldn't.

I didn't think anyone could.

You never forget your first love. And you never forget when someone betrays you. How did you cope when it was the same person?

Logan touched my hand. "I felt that she'd been toying with me the entire time we were together. We had a fight in my cabin, and when she left that was the last time I ever saw her. When I heard she was missing, I was shocked. I couldn't believe it. How could she just disappear? I kept hoping she was going to be found, but with each passing day, my hope faded, replaced by something else."

"What?"

"Fear," he whispered. "She might have broken my heart, but I didn't want her dead. That's the other reason why I don't like talking about her. I don't want to think that she might not be alive. She was too young to die. When I think of Taylor, I want to remember the happy times. I want to remember her laughing and smiling. Before all the bad stuff happened."

"Do you think she's dead?" I asked.

Logan shrugged. "She has to be, don't you think?"

"I don't know," I said in answer to his question.

"They searched the ship from top to bottom. The only explanation anyone has been able to come up with is that she fell overboard." Logan sighed. "Is there anything else you want to know about her?"

"No." I'd heard everything I needed to hear about Taylor.

"Then let's not talk about her again, okay? I still can't process what happened so I try not to think about it. Taylor's a part of my life that I want to forget."

"But have you?" I asked.

Logan gave me a smile. "Yes, I have." He kissed me. "Because of you."

"I didn't mean to hurt you by bringing up her name," I said, wrapping my arms around him and snuggling up against his chest. "The only reason I brought up Taylor is because I don't want you to think I'm like her. I'm not. And I'm not going to hurt you. I promise."

Logan gazed down at me and shook his head sadly. "You shouldn't make promises you can't keep, Ashley. Don't you know it's dangerous to do that?"

Chapter 14

When we got back to the cruise ship later that afternoon, I asked Logan if he wanted to have dinner together. Our day had been perfect and I wanted to end it with a romantic evening for two. I imagined us gazing into each other's eyes over lit candles, holding hands, and then maybe I'd rub my foot up his leg under the table before things really heated up and we decided to go off for our own dessert.

"I wish I could, but I can't," he said. "I have to work tonight."

I tried not to look disappointed, but it was hard. I loved spending time with Logan. Now I wouldn't see him until his shift was finished.

"I'm off tomorrow night. How 'bout if we go back to the island for dinner?"

I gave him a smile. "It's a date!"

"Want to take a dip in the pool now?" he suggested. "I've got some time before I have to get to the dining room."

The pool area wasn't as crowded as it usually was. A lot of people had gone sightseeing. Logan found us two lounge chairs together.

"Want something to drink?" he asked after dumping his stuff.

"A lemonade would really hit the spot."

"You got it."

While Logan went to get our drinks, I jumped into the pool. The water felt cool and refreshing as it washed away the sand, sweat, and sunblock that was all over my body. I was toweling off when Logan came back with our drinks.

"One lemonade," Logan said, handing me a glass.

I took a sip and shivered. The lemonade was sweet and tart, just the way I like it. "Thanks."

Logan took off his tank top and then dived into the pool. I watched as he swam from one end to the other, his lean body cutting through the water. I couldn't take my eyes off him.

"Whatcha looking at?" he asked as he came

out of the water, his body glistening with droplets of water, and plopped onto the chaise lounge next to me.

"You."

"Like what you see?" he asked.

"Uh-huh."

He lay down on his chair, putting his sunglasses back on his face. "So tell me about your ex-boyfriend."

I was caught completely off-guard. Logan turned on his side to face me, propping up his elbow and resting his chin in the palm of his hand. "You don't mind, do you?"

"How could I?" He had told me all about Taylor. I couldn't refuse.

"What do you want to know?" I asked.

Logan shrugged. "I don't know. Fill in the blanks."

"Finn and I dated for a couple of months. He walked me home one day, asked me out, and the next thing I knew we were a couple."

"But what drew you to him in the first place? What kept the two of you together?"

Good question. I'd been asking myself that very same question the last couple of weeks.

"Finn was the guy that every girl in my high school wanted to go out with, including me," I said. "And I was the one who caught his attention. I was the one he walked home and I was the one he asked out. When the most popular guy at your high school asks you out, you don't say no. You say yes! And I did. Over and over again."

"Lucky Finn," Logan said.

"In the beginning, I was caught up in being with Finn," I continued. "Out of all the girls in our high school, he had asked *me* out. Me! I couldn't believe it. We went everywhere together. But we were always going to parties, always hanging out with his friends and not mine. There was never any alone time for the two of us and when there was, we always did what Finn wanted to do. It was all about Finn. Never about *us*. After a while, I got tired of it." I shrugged. "We just weren't a good fit. I wanted something real and Finn didn't. I should have broken up with him sooner, but I didn't."

"I'm glad you finally did."

I gave Logan a smile as I took another sip of my lemonade. "So am I."

"Do you still have feelings for him?"

I coughed on my lemonade. "What kind of question is that?"

"What? Sometimes couples break up and get back together. It's hard to turn off feelings."

"Trust me, I feel absolutely nothing for Finn. Nothing. It's over between us," I stated firmly. "All I want is to be with someone who wants to be with me. I thought that person was Finn, but I was wrong. I'm not saying we didn't have fun together. Finn can be romantic when he wants to be. I guess I was hoping he was my Prince Charming."

I ran a finger over the rim of my lemonade glass. "I've always been a sucker for fairy tales," I admitted. "Snow White. Cinderella. Sleeping Beauty. I'm not saying I need to be *rescued*, but there was someone waiting for them. Their own special someone."

"Is that what you want?" Logan asked. "Your own special someone?"

"Yes," I confessed, looking up at Logan. "I want my own special someone."

Logan leaned forward and gave me a kiss. "I think you found him."

⁂

Logan and I spent an hour at the pool. Thankfully, there were no more questions about Finn. Instead, we talked about our favorite movies (I loved old romantic comedies like *Sabrina* and *Breakfast at Tiffany's*, as well as new ones like *SuperBad* and *The Devil Wears Prada*, while Logan was addicted to old monster movies, especially the Godzilla ones), TV shows (I was a reality TV junkie—LOVED *America's Next Top Model*, and even its cheesy spin-offs—while Logan liked watching the Sci-Fi Channel), books (I was a huge Meg Cabot fan while Logan loved Stephen King and Dean Koontz; we both LOVED J. K. Rowling), and anything else we could think of.

When it was time for Logan to head back to his cabin to get ready for work, he gave me a good-bye kiss. It was a sweet, gentle kiss—the kind a boyfriend gives his girlfriend when he has to leave her and doesn't want to.

"How about we go dancing later tonight?" he asked.

"Sounds like fun."

After Logan left, I stayed at the pool for

another fifteen minutes before heading back to my cabin. When I got there, I found a note from Charlotte, telling me that she and Sam were going to have dinner in Nassau.

After taking a shower, I decided to dress simply. I'd gotten some color on the beach so I went with a yellow sundress. The yellow showed off my tan, and the bracelet that Logan bought me went perfectly with it.

At dinner—we were at the ship's Italian dining room tonight, La Strada—Simone, Kristine, and I compared notes on our day. I had to compliment them on their outfits. They both looked *so* adorable. Simone was in a purple striped halter-neck dress while Kristine was wearing a white dress that left one of her shoulders bare.

They had gone snorkeling along a coral reef and then did some shopping. Naturally, Simone wanted to hear all about Logan. At first I teased her, not saying much, before finally confessing all.

"Do you think he might be *the one*?" she asked.

She was asking if Logan might be the first

guy I sleep with. "I don't know," I said, moving around the baby red potatoes on my plate. "Maybe. I'm not going to rush into anything."

"Take your time," Kristine advised me, glaring at Simone like she was a bad influence.

Simone ignored Kristine. "I've never seen you talk about a guy the way you do about Logan."

She was right. I didn't know what it was. Maybe chemistry.

Or maybe it was love.

Love?

After three days? Maybe it was love at first sight.

I didn't know.

All I knew was that I wanted to spend as much time with Logan as I possibly could. I couldn't wait until I saw him later.

We skipped dessert and headed straight to Club Paradise. It was seventies-eighties night and the soundtrack to *Saturday Night Fever* was playing. We ran out onto the dance floor and started boogeying to "Staying Alive."

Charlotte and Sam showed up while we

were dancing to Blondie's "Call Me." When the song was over, I went to where Charlotte was sitting on the side, watching the dancers. Sam was already dancing by himself. And not very well! But he was having a good time and that's what mattered, I guess.

"Aren't you going to dance?" I asked her.

"In a little bit. How was your day?"

I told Charlotte everything about my day with Logan. I wanted to start confiding in her so that she would start confiding in me, like real sisters.

"Sounds like things are really heating up between the two of you," she said.

"They are."

"This beach sounds so romantic! Where is it again? Maybe Sam and I will head out there tomorrow."

I gave Charlotte directions and then headed back out onto the dance floor as a new song started. I had just begun dancing when the last person I wanted to see planted himself in front of me.

It was Finn.

"I want to talk to you," he said.

"About what?"

"Us."

"There is no *us*," I said, turning my back on him. I wanted to leave the dance floor, but I wasn't going to let Finn ruin my night.

Finn placed an arm on my shoulder and spun me around.

"I don't want to talk to you!" I snapped, still angry over the stunt he and Tabitha had pulled the night before. Okay, I had no proof it was them, but who else could it have been? "I don't have anything to say to you. Just leave me alone!"

"How can you do this to me?" he asked, confusion written all over his face. "I don't understand. Give me an explanation. We were the perfect couple."

"Maybe *you* thought we were the perfect couple, but we weren't." For a while, in those first weeks when we had started dating, I had thought we were the perfect couple too. How could I not? I was one of the most popular girls at our high school and he was one of the most popular guys. Everyone wanted to be us. But there's more to life than being popular. There had been nothing *real* about our relationship.

"Tell me what I did wrong and I'll fix it," Finn said. "I'm sorry about the joke. I'll never do something like that again."

"It's too late to fix things."

"Let me try," he said. "Why won't you let me try?"

"Because I don't want to be with you anymore!" I shouted, my patience gone. "How many times do I have to say it?"

"You'd rather be with that waiter?" Finn sneered. "Do you know how everyone is going to laugh at me when they find out you dumped me for a waiter?"

So that was what this was all about. Finn's pride! He didn't care about me. It was all about his image.

"You're pathetic," I said, getting ready to leave the dance floor as a love song started.

"Not so fast," he said, pulling me into his arms and holding me close. "One last dance. For old times' sake."

I tried to break free, but I couldn't. He was too strong. I glanced around the dance floor, searching for Simone or Kristine to help me. I even searched for Charlotte and Sam, but no one was around.

Finn kept me locked tight against his body, whispering into my ear. "You're making a mistake," he said.

I refused to answer him. All I wanted was for the song to end. When it finally did, I thought he would let me go, but he didn't. While we were dancing, he had steered us into a dark corner of the dance floor. When the music ended, he backed me into the corner and kissed me.

"I thought you said it was over between the two of you," a voice from behind us said.

Logan!

I looked over Finn's shoulder and saw Logan staring at me with a stunned expression on his face.

Then he turned around and walked away.

I tried to break free of Finn's hold so I could run after him. I almost got away, but Finn caught me by the wrist that had Logan's bracelet on it.

"Logan!" I called, trying not to sound frantic. "Wait!"

But he didn't.

He just kept walking.

"Let me go!" I shouted to Finn, struggling to free my wrist. As I did, my bracelet broke and seashells went scattering to the floor, smashing into tiny pieces.

"Look at what you did!" I screamed in horror.

I stared at the broken pieces of seashells strewn on the dance floor, wondering if my new romance was just as broken.

I searched all over the ship but I couldn't find Logan. I even knocked on his cabin door but there was no answer. Either he was inside and pretending not to be there or he was somewhere else. Simone and Kristine were searching with me, while Charlotte and Sam were searching together.

"It doesn't look like we're going to find him tonight," Kristine said.

Simone checked the time on her watch.

"We've been searching for over an hour. It's almost one."

"You'll talk to him in the morning," Kristine said.

"This can't wait until the morning," I said. "I have to talk to him tonight. You didn't see the look on his face. He was so hurt. I know he was comparing me to her."

"Who?" Kristine asked.

"Taylor! He thinks I'm just like her, that I'm juggling two boyfriends. He even asked me at the pool today if I still had feelings for Finn. Then he caught me kissing him."

"You weren't kissing him," Simone said. "Finn was forcing himself on you. There's a big difference."

"But Logan doesn't know that!"

"He will after you explain it all to him," Simone said reassuringly.

"Come on, Ashley," Kristine said, wrapping an arm around my shoulders and leading me in the direction of my cabin. "You need to go to bed."

"Do you want us to spend the night with

you?" Simone asked.

I shook my head. "No, I'm okay. But thanks for the offer."

"Everything will be fine in the morning," Kristine vowed as they said good night. "You'll see."

After Kristine and Simone left, I tried to go to sleep but I couldn't. I kept thinking of Logan. We'd had such a wonderful day and it had ended horribly.

I only hoped he would give me a second chance.

The following morning when I woke up, I found a note in a white envelope slipped under my cabin door. The front of the envelope was blank.

I opened the envelope and read the note inside: *MEET ME ON THE BEACH.*

My heart began pounding with excitement.

Logan wanted to talk about the night before at our special, romantic spot on the beach.

He was giving me a second chance!

As I got dressed, I noticed Charlotte's bed

was still made. She must have spent the night with Sam again.

Once I'd made it to Nassau, I hopped on a bus to the beach.

It was as deserted and private as it had been the day before. I walked to our spot under the cliffs and waited.

As I waited, I wondered what I would say to Logan. I only hoped he would believe the truth.

The beach was quiet except for the occasional screech of a seagull. I glanced at the time on my watch. I'd already been waiting for over an hour. Where was he?

Just then, I heard something.

It sounded like rumbling.

Thunder?

I looked up at the sky and gasped.

Falling straight at me from the top of the cliff was a huge boulder!

Chapter 15

I felt stunned in place but managed to scramble to one side and watch as the boulder smashed into the sand where I had been standing only seconds before.

If I hadn't looked up . . .

If I hadn't jumped out of the way . . .

I could have been killed.

My knees buckled with fear and I fell to the sand.

I must have passed out because the next thing I knew, I could feel my face being dabbed with a wet handkerchief. My eyes fluttered open and I saw the concerned faces of an elderly man and woman. They were wearing khaki cargo shorts, blue flip-flops, and bright red T-shirts that read *WE PARTIED IN THE BAHAMAS!* I struggled to sit up.

"What happened?" I asked, placing a hand over my eyes so I could shade them from the sun.

"You were almost hit by that," the man said, pointing to the boulder.

I stared at the boulder and the memory of my close call instantly came back. I shuddered.

"You must have passed out for a few seconds," the woman said, helping me stand up. "I'm Mamie and this is my husband, Harold." She held out her water bottle. "Would you like a sip?"

"No thanks." My stomach was still doing somersaults and I didn't think I'd be putting anything in it for a while.

"You were very lucky," Mamie said, her voice filled with concern. "If you hadn't jumped out of the way, you could have been seriously injured. Or worse."

"I know," I whispered as I realized again how close I had come to dying.

"Are you okay?" Harold asked, peering at me from behind the thick lenses of his glasses. His brown eyes were super-magnified, making him look like a cartoon owl. "Do you want us to take you to a doctor?"

"I'm fine," I said, brushing sand off the bottom of my shorts. "Really."

Mamie held her handkerchief to her water bottle and dabbed my face again. The water felt nice against my flushed skin. The sun was already out and blazing hotly. "What are you doing out here all by yourself so early in the morning?"

"I was meeting someone. But he never showed up." I wondered where Logan was. Why had he sent me that note if he hadn't intended to meet me? Had this been his idea of a joke?

"Hmph!" Mamie said, scowling. "Some friend. Making you come all the way out here and not showing up. If he'd shown up when he was supposed to, maybe this accident wouldn't have happened."

"But it did," I whispered, staring at the boulder and realizing how lucky I was to still be alive. "It did."

Harold and Mamie insisted on bringing me to the dock, leaving me once I was in a tender on my way back to the ship. They waved at me as

I pulled away and I waved back, giving them a smile so they'd think I was fine, even though I wasn't fine at all.

My mind was racing. If it hadn't been for Logan and his note, I never would have been on that beach. I wouldn't have almost been killed. If I hadn't moved out of the way, I could have been lying on that beach for hours, slowly dying.

As the tender got closer and closer to the ship, I became angrier and angrier. Logan was going to have a lot of explaining to do!

After getting back on the ship, I went searching for him. I found him in the English Muffin, piling dirty breakfast dishes on a tray.

"Where were you?" I demanded, not giving him a chance to talk and catching him off-guard. I could see that he was surprised by the anger in my voice. "I waited for over an hour and you never showed up. I was almost killed because of you!"

"Killed?" Concern filled his voice. "What are you talking about? What happened?"

"Like you really care! If you had shown up like you were supposed to, maybe none of this would have happened!"

"I don't know what you're talking about," he said, confusion in his voice.

"You were supposed to meet me on the beach."

"I was?"

"You left me a note, remember?'

"I didn't send you any note."

"What do you mean you didn't send me a note?" If I'd had the note on me, I would have waved it in his face. But I didn't. I had thrown it out after reading it. "You slipped it under my door this morning!"

Logan folded his arms over his chest. "Was my name on it?"

What did that have to do with anything? "No," I said.

"Then how do you know it was from me?"

"It said, 'Meet me on the beach.' We spent the day on the beach yesterday. I just assumed it was from you."

He began stacking juice glasses on top of one another. "It wasn't."

I pulled out a chair and sank into it. Now I was the one who was confused. If Logan hadn't sent me the note, then who had?

Why would someone ask me to meet them on the beach?

A niggling thought started forming. A horrible thought.

What if I had been brought to the beach for a reason?

What if the boulder hadn't fallen by accident?

What if someone had pushed it over the edge on purpose?

To make it *look* like an accident?

But who?

I stared at Logan, eyes widening.

What if he *had* sent me the note? What if he was lying about not sending it?

What if after seeing me last night with Finn, he'd decided to get even?

After all, Taylor had disappeared as soon as they'd had a fight.

Stop it! I scolded myself. *Stop it!* Was I suffering from heatstroke?! Logan did not try to kill me! He did *not* have anything to do with Taylor's disappearance. I was being paranoid because I was such an emotional mess.

Logan sat in the chair next to me. "Ashley, tell me what happened," he said. "Please. I can see that you're upset."

"Okay."

When I finished telling Logan my story, all the color drained from his face. He looked scared.

"You were lucky," he said. "Very lucky."

"I know."

"If anything had happened to you, I don't know what I would have done. Especially after last night." He looked down at his hands, then back at me. "I actually wanted to talk to you about last night. I'm sorry I didn't stay and hear you out. Kristine and Simone found me this morning and they explained what happened with Finn. I shouldn't have believed what I saw. I shouldn't have doubted you." He sighed. "I should have trusted you."

"Yes, you should have."

"I think you know why I have an issue with trust. I need to put the past behind me." Logan looked me in the eye. "Yesterday you said you wanted your own special someone. That's me, Ashley. The reason why I was so upset is because I think I'm falling in love with you."

Those were the last words I had expected to hear. My heart melted. "You are?" I whispered in surprise. No guy had ever told me he loved me. It gave me a warm and fuzzy feeling inside. It made me feel special. Very special.

"I am."

I instantly felt ashamed for thinking Logan had had anything to do with the falling boulder. How could I have doubted him for even a second?

But then I remembered the note.

The note had made me doubt him.

Someone had slipped it under my door.

Someone had wanted me on the beach.

Since it hadn't been Logan who left it, then it had to be someone else.

It didn't take me long to come up with a list of names.

Finn.

Tabitha.

Sam.

"You're still thinking about that note, aren't

you?" Logan asked, breaking into my thoughts.

"I'm trying to figure out who could have sent it."

"Was your name on the front of the envelope? Was it addressed to you?"

I thought back. "Actually, no. It wasn't. The front of the envelope was blank."

"Then maybe it was meant for Charlotte," Logan suggested. "Maybe Sam sent it. Or maybe it was meant for someone else and slipped under the wrong door."

Could that be all it was? I wondered. Logan's theory *did* make sense.

"So you're saying it was just wrong place, wrong time?"

"Absolutely." Logan pulled my chair closer to his and leaned over to give me a kiss. "After all, who would want to hurt you?"

I thought about Logan's question.

And I couldn't find an answer.

Finn might be angry at me for breaking up with him and not giving him a second chance, but would he really try to hurt me? Once we returned home and it got out that he was back on the market, he was going to have girls all over him. And while Tabitha and I had had our fights over the years, she'd never been dangerous. As for Sam, he only weirded me out. That wasn't a crime.

Just because I suspected someone of doing something didn't mean that they had.

You couldn't accuse someone without proof.

And I didn't have any.

Everything that had happened in the last couple of days had been freaky accidents. I was making it out to be more than it was because of an overactive imagination. I needed to rein it in!

"So what would you say to a romantic dinner for two tonight in Nassau?" Logan asked. "It's our last night here before we set sail in the morning."

"I'd say yes!"

"Be ready to leave the ship at six." Logan glanced at the table of dirty dishes next to us. "I'd better get back to work."

I hopped to my feet. "Speaking of work, you're still coming to my Sweet Sixteen party later in the week, right? You don't have to work that night, do you?"

"I wouldn't miss it. I already swapped shifts with a friend. Now all I have to do is find you a present."

"I don't need a present," I said, moving close and wrapping my arms around his neck. "Having you there is enough."

"Every birthday girl deserves a present," Logan said, smiling at me mysteriously. "I want to find you something really special. Something to die for!"

And then he kissed me. A long, sweet kiss that had my pulse racing and my heart melting.

You're such an idiot, I told myself as I walked away later. *How could you have even suspected Logan of doing anything wrong? No one who kisses like this could be dangerous.*

Chapter 16

I felt much better after talking to Logan. After leaving him, I tracked down Simone, Kristine, and Charlotte, asking them to meet me at the ship's costume shop in thirty minutes. There was going to be a masquerade ball the following night and we needed to pick out costumes.

I got to the shop first and began going through the racks. There was so much to choose from! I wasn't sure what I wanted to go as, but I wanted it to be something fun.

I had just added a belly dancer outfit to the pile of costumes I'd chosen to try on when Simone and Kristine arrived.

"I love costume parties," Kristine gushed, flipping through the costumes draped over my arm.

"Where were you this morning?" Simone

asked. "We knocked on your door but there was no answer."

"I was looking for Logan," I said, deciding not to tell them about my beach excursion. It was over and done with. There was no need to rehash it or worry them. I'd done enough silly worrying for all of us.

"We should have figured that," Kristine said, holding up a witch's costume before putting it back. "Ugh! Too ugly!"

"Thanks for talking to him," I said. "We patched things up."

Kristine clapped her hands happily. "Yay!"

"You made up with Logan?" Charlotte asked as she came into the costume shop. Trailing behind her was Sam. Luckily, he went to explore the men's costumes, leaving us alone for girl talk. "That's great news!"

"Oooh! I'm going to try this one on!" Kristine exclaimed, zeroing in on a costume and running off to the dressing rooms.

"What do you think?" she asked a few minutes later, rejoining us. She was dressed as a mermaid, wearing a bikini top made of glittering sea-green crystals. The bottom was a long skintight skirt that fanned out in the shape of a fin. On her head was a long red wig that almost touched the floor.

"Are you supposed to be the Little Mermaid?" Simone laughed as she disappeared into a dressing room with a costume of her own.

"The Little Mermaid?" Kristine gasped. "I don't want to go as her! Guys don't find the Little Mermaid hot!"

"Ignore her," I told Kristine. "You look great. Very sexy! But isn't that hard to walk in?"

"Good point," Kristine said as she took tiny steps back to the dressing room. "I'll find something else."

"How about this for me?" Simone asked as she walked out.

She was dressed as Wonder Woman.

"Figures you would go with something short and revealing," I said.

"It shows off my body, don't you think?" she asked, admiring herself in a full-length mirror as she adjusted the gold headband in her hair. "I need to do *something*. This cruise is almost half over and I haven't met anyone yet!" She turned to Sam, who had wandered over. "What do you think of my costume, Sam?"

Simone's question caused Sam to blush. "You look nice."

Simone pouted. "Just nice?"

"If you wear that, you're going to have to beat the guys away."

Simone gave Sam a big smile. "*That* was the answer I was hoping for! So, what are you going as?"

"I haven't found a costume yet."

"You need something sexy too. I bet you have muscles hidden under those loose T-shirts you always wear."

"I do work out," Sam admitted, blushing again.

"I can tell! We need to show off those muscles!" She took him by the hand. "Come on. Let's go see if we can find you a gladiator costume. Gladiators are sexy."

"That'd be great," Sam said as he followed after Simone.

I could tell Charlotte didn't like the banter going on between Sam and Simone. She had shot them both dark looks, but they were oblivious. Charlotte's jealousy surprised me. I had never seen that side of her before.

"What are you thinking of wearing, Charlotte?" I asked, trying to distract her. She really didn't have anything to worry about. I couldn't see Simone making a play for Sam.

She showed me a nun's outfit. It was black and shapeless, with long, voluminous sleeves and a huge headdress for her head.

My mouth dropped open. "You're kidding, right?"

"What's wrong with it?" she asked.

"You're going to be completely covered up!" I exclaimed. "From head to toe! The only thing we'll be able to see is your face."

"I think it's kind of fun. I can look all stern and scary and wave a ruler in everyone's face."

How oblivious was my sister when it came to guys? Obviously, Sam was more into Wonder Woman. She needed to lighten up.

I tried to steer Charlotte toward the sexier costumes, but she didn't want to try any of them on. I quickly learned that when my sister makes up her mind, that's it. You can't change it.

I finally gave up and went to try on my costumes. The one I liked most was the belly dancer outfit. The strapless top was covered with fake jewels and sparkles while the pants were made of silk. On my feet I wore slippers with curled toes, and a sheer veil covered the lower part of my face. On top of my head I wore a brunette wig that had a huge bun and coiled braids wrapped around it.

I danced out of my dressing room with my arms over my head.

"What do you think?" I asked.

"I love it!" Kristine exclaimed. She held up a costume. "I'm going as a ballerina."

Simone walked over to me, nodding at my costume in approval. "We weren't able to find a gladiator costume, but I think Sammy looks cute as a boxer, don't you?"

I noticed that Sam was wearing a pair of red satin shorts and had boxing gloves on his hands.

"We'll wet him down with some water, add a little fake blood on his face, and he'll look like he just stepped out of a ring," Simone said.

"Sammy?" I whispered to Simone.

I wasn't the only one who'd heard the

nickname. Charlotte had too. And she was scowling at Simone.

Simone lowered her voice. "With a little work, Poindexter could actually be a hottie."

"Poindexter is taken," I reminded Simone.

"I know, I know. I'm just saying."

Simone's never gone after another girl's guy, and I didn't think she was going to start now. But Charlotte didn't know that. And she'd had enough. She stormed over to Simone. If she'd had that ruler, she'd be waving it in Simone's face.

"Thanks for your help, Simone," she said. "But Sam's costume is all wrong."

"Really? I think he looks pretty good in it."

Charlotte shook her head. "Well, I don't. And if anyone knows Sam, it's me, his girlfriend."

"I was only trying to help," Simone said.

Charlotte turned to Sam. "You don't like that costume, do you, Sam?"

Poor Sam. I actually felt sorry for him. He looked like an escaped prisoner caught under a bright spotlight. I could tell that he liked the boxer costume. But at the same time, he could see how upset Charlotte was.

"Do you?" she insisted when he still wouldn't answer.

"I think I should try on a couple more costumes before making up my mind," he said carefully. "Why don't you help me pick some out?"

"See?" Charlotte crowed to Simone as she grabbed Sam by the arm and led him to the front of the store.

"Who knew Char was so touchy?" Simone asked.

"Can you blame her?" I asked. "You were flirting with her boyfriend!"

I hurried into the dressing room to change back into my clothes. When I got out, Charlotte and Sam were gone.

"Did everyone remember to get eye masks?" Kristine asked as the cashier swiped our card keys and charged our costume rentals to our rooms. "We're supposed to wear them until midnight. That's when everyone is unmasked."

"What's the point?" Simone asked. "We already know what we're all going as."

"I included eye masks with everyone's

costumes," the cashier told us as she handed us our costumes in boxes. "You're all set."

"You have to wear your eye mask," I told Simone. "It's all part of the fun. Promise that you will?"

"Okay, okay," Simone grumbled. "It's going to ruin my makeup, but I'll do it."

"My tan needs a little bit of a boost," Kristine said, peering at her arms and legs. "Why don't we drop off our costumes in our cabins and then spend the rest of the day by the pool?"

"Sounds good to me," I agreed. "See you in a bit."

I was walking back to my cabin when I ran into Molly. I gave her a smile, but she didn't smile back.

"There you are!" she hissed. "I've been looking all over for you. I've got something to say to you!"

I was taken aback by her anger. What had I done?

"How dare you treat Logan the way you did last night! Especially after everything I told you about him and how Taylor broke his heart. You're no different than she was."

Logan must have told Molly what had happened with Finn, but she hadn't seen him since we'd made up.

"Molly! Wait!" I said, holding up a hand so she'd let me talk. "Let me explain!"

"There's nothing to explain," she said. "You're horrible. Just like she was!"

"Molly, nothing happened last night. It wasn't what it looked like."

Molly stared at me like I was crazy. "What do you mean? Logan caught you kissing Finn."

"Finn was kissing me," I clarified. "I wasn't kissing him."

I told Molly everything about the night before and about how Logan and I had patched things up. When I finished talking, Molly ran her fingers through her hair and yanked on it.

"Argh! I feel like such an idiot. I'm so sorry I flew off the handle at you. It's just that Logan is special to me, you know? He's my friend."

I did know. If someone hurt one of my friends, I'd be out for blood.

"Logan's really lucky to have you watching his back," I said.

"He's a great guy." She groaned. "I'm so embarrassed!"

I wanted to show Molly there were no hard feelings.

"I'm having a Sweet Sixteen party later in the week," I told her. "I'd love it if you could come."

"It's *so* sweet of you to invite me," she said. "Especially after the way I was all in your face."

I waved a hand in the air. "That's all over and done with. So come to my party, okay?"

She gave me a smile. "A party would be fun. It'll be something to look forward to."

"Aren't you going to the masquerade ball tomorrow night?"

Molly shook her head. "No."

"How come? Do you have to work?"

"I can't afford to rent a costume," she confessed. "I'm saving every last cent I make for my college fund."

An idea suddenly popped into my head. I

looked at Molly. She and I were about the same size.

"Would you be willing to help me out with something?"

"What?"

"I want to play a joke on my friends."

"What kind of joke?"

"Nothing major," I assured her. "My friends already know what my costume is going to be for the ball, but I want to get another one and fool them. If you wear my costume, they'll think it's me. With a new costume that no one knows about, I'll be almost invisible. I could have some fun with them, and they wouldn't even know it was me!"

"Oooh, I love practical jokes," Molly squealed.

"So you'll do it?"

"Sure!" Molly exclaimed as I handed her the box with my costume in it. "This is going to be fun!"

"Don't forget to wear your eye mask!" I reminded her. "We can't fool them if they see your face."

After I left Molly I went back to the costume

shop and found the other costume I had really liked. It was a wedding gown that had a thick veil. Between that and my eye mask, no one was going to be able to recognize me!

After the sales clerk boxed up my costume, I hurried back to my cabin. I was running late and I was sure Simone and Kristine were wondering where I was.

I changed into a swimsuit and then I went to put my costume in the closet.

When I opened the closet door, I found a nasty surprise.

I gasped, my eyes blinking in disbelief as I dropped the box with my costume.

I couldn't be seeing what I was seeing.

My birthday dress was completely slashed!

Chapter 17

*A*t first I thought my eyes were playing tricks on me.

But then I reached for the hanger, taking the dress out of the closet, holding it in front of me.

I stared at the slashed strips of fabric.

Then I touched them, my fingers slowly fluttering through them.

It was real.

Someone had hacked my dress with either a knife or an open pair of scissors.

It was ruined.

Destroyed.

Who could have done such a thing?

I dropped the dress to the floor. Why was I even asking myself that question?

Tabitha!

She had wanted this dress and, since she couldn't have it, she'd decided I couldn't have it, either.

She'd gotten into my cabin once before and now she had done it again!

This time she had gone too far.

And I wasn't going to let her get away with it.

"Where've you been?" Kristine asked as I approached the pool area. "Simone's got her eye on the lifeguard and she needs to figure out a strategy."

"Should I do the fake drowning thing?" Simone asked. "I'd love some mouth-to-mouth with that cutie."

I didn't answer them. I was too focused on Tabitha, who was at the far end of the pool on a chaise lounge. Finn was nowhere in sight. She was wearing a peach crocheted bikini and a pair of oversized sunglasses with white frames. She didn't see me coming and I wanted the element of surprise.

"Hey!" Kristine called out after me as I walked past her and didn't stop. "Where are you going?"

I still didn't answer her. Instead, I closed the distance between myself and Tabitha. With each step I took, my anger grew. I didn't know what I was going to do, but I wanted it to be something Tabitha wouldn't forget.

Her chaise lounge was close to the edge of the pool. Impulsively, I lifted up the side of it and tossed her into the pool, watching as she fell into the water.

"Hey!" she shouted as she resurfaced, pushing her sunglasses to the top of her head and gasping for air. "What's wrong with you?" she asked, her voice filled with outrage.

"Why did you do it?" I shouted.

Kristine ran to my side, shock written all over her face. "Ashley! What's going on?"

Simone was right behind her. "Ashley?"

Neither one of them had ever seen this side of me before. I never lost my temper and I never started fights.

Tabitha swam to the side of the pool and started climbing up the ladder. "Do what?"

"Don't play dumb with me, *Tabby*," I said, waiting to meet her as she got out of the pool and following after her. "You know what I'm talking about."

Tabitha rolled her eyes. "Are you going to accuse me of doing something I didn't do again? This game of yours is getting tired, *Ash*." She glanced at Kristine and Simone. "I think your best friend needs some mental help. She's losing it."

Tabitha flipped her chaise lounge back on its legs and reached into her beach bag for a towel. She began drying herself off.

"You know what you did," I told her. "You slashed my dress. The dress you couldn't buy. I found it hanging in my closet where you left it for me."

Kristine gasped. "No!"

"That was going way too far, Tabitha, even for you," Simone said.

Tabitha threw her towel down. "Why would I slash her stupid dress?" she asked angrily.

"Because I had it and you didn't and that pissed you off," I said.

"You're crazy, you know that? I didn't touch

your stupid dress."

"If you didn't do it, then who else would?" I demanded.

"Someone else who hates you," Tabitha answered.

Her words were like a slap in the face.

"What's the matter, Ashley? Shocked?" She smirked. "You think everyone loves you. Well, here's a news flash. They don't."

"That's not true," Kristine said, rushing to my defense. "Everyone loves Ashley."

"Everyone she hangs out with does. But how about the girls who aren't invited to her parties? Or the guys she turns down? Or the ones whose fathers can't afford to send them on a birthday cruise for their Sweet Sixteen? They don't love her. They *despise* her. And Ashley thinks she's too good for them."

"That's not true!" I shouted.

I wasn't like those Mean Girls at most high schools. The ones who ran together in packs and made fun of the girls who weren't in their group. The ones who pulled humiliating jokes on the guys who were nerds or the girls who weren't as pretty as they were. I tried to be nice to everyone. What was so wrong with hanging out with the same people all the time? They were my friends!

"It is!" Tabitha shouted back. "You just don't want to admit it."

"Even if what you say is true, none of those people are on this ship," I said. "But *you* are."

Tabitha gave a nasty laugh. "You don't think people on this ship haven't noticed what a spoiled little princess you are? Any one of them could have slashed your dress."

I didn't want to believe it. Tabitha was messing with my head. The loose railing. The falling boulder. Those were all freaky accidents. But the message on my bathroom mirror and my slashed dress? Someone had done those things and that someone was Tabitha. I didn't care what she said.

"It wasn't anyone else," I insisted. "It was you. And if you do something like that to me again, you're going to regret it. I'm warning you, Tabitha. Stay away from me."

I had hoped by the time my date with Logan arrived I would have been over the shock of finding my dress slashed. But I wasn't. And Logan noticed.

"What's with the frown?" he asked as we took our seats in the Nassau restaurant. Logan had chosen a local spot where we could taste all sorts of native dishes. The décor of the restaurant was very laid-back. The walls were painted a bright yellow, there were potted palm trees decorated with coconuts, and the tables were covered with light blue tablecloths and handmade straw place mats. Sand was scattered over the hardwood floor. It was like having a little slice of paradise indoors.

"I've been doing all the talking," he said as our waiter handed us our menus. They were parchment and the selections were written in calligraphy. "You've hardly said a word."

Even though I didn't want to rehash the whole thing again, I told Logan about my ruined dress.

"You really think Tabitha did it?"

"If she didn't, then who did? I can't think of anyone else."

I was also bothered by what Tabitha had

said about people hating me, but I didn't want to tell Logan. I didn't want him to think that it could be true. It wasn't! Even though I didn't socialize outside my clique, I wasn't the only one. That's just the way it is with cliques. You hang out with the people you have the most in common with. But maybe my actions were sending an entirely different message. Maybe I needed to start socializing with other groups at my high school.

Although I hated to admit it, Tabitha's words did make me realize that when it came to dating, I hadn't looked outside my social circle. I only went out with guys who my friends and I hung out with. It wasn't something I had consciously done. Finn was the perfect example. He had been popular and I had been popular. At the time, everyone, including me, had thought we were the perfect match because of that.

But we weren't.

And now, happily, Logan was the exception to my dating pattern.

Maybe I should start applying that thinking to other areas of my life.

"You look nice," Logan said, cutting into my thoughts.

I was wearing a peach wrap dress with strappy high-heeled sandals. Logan was wearing plaid Bermuda shorts, an orange-and-tan-striped polo shirt, and a light brown cotton jacket with the sleeves pushed up. Our colors matched and I thought we looked very much like a couple.

"I can tell you're still thinking about Tabitha," Logan said. "Let it go."

I ran a hand through my hair, tossing it over one shoulder. "I can't put my finger on what it is, but something about this is bothering me," I admitted.

"You don't think she did it?"

"Tabitha was so adamant that she didn't slash my dress. We've never gotten along, but we've always been more like frenemies than true enemies. In all our years of fighting, she's never done anything so nasty and vindictive."

Logan shrugged. "She finally showed her true colors."

"I guess."

Logan reached for my hand across the table. "Let's forget about Tabitha and have a good time."

When our waiter arrived, I trusted Logan to do all the ordering. We started with two dishes made from conch. Conch was a local shellfish and the beach was scattered with their empty pink shells. They were the type of shell that you put against your ear to hear the sound of waves. The conch chowder was spicy and made with vegetables while the conch fritters were pieces of chopped-up conch rolled in flour and herbs and then fried. I never say no to anything fried!

After that we had shredded lobster with green peppers, tomatoes, and onions. As a side dish we had johnnycake, which is a sweet bread. We topped it all off with coconut tarts for dessert.

After dinner, we walked back to the dock, holding hands. We were quiet, not talking, just enjoying being with each other. I couldn't remember the last time I'd had such a great date.

As we were walking along, Logan stopped

in front of a shop. The window was filled with an array of touristy type things like T-shirts, postcards, seashells, and ceramics. "Do you mind if I pop in here for a second? I'll be really quick." He gave me a quick kiss before I could answer and dashed inside.

Chapter 18

I was going to follow after Logan when a skirt with a tropical design caught my eye in a shop across the street.

I peeked into the store Logan was in and saw it was crowded with customers. I bet he'd be in there for a while. I probably had time to go across the street, ask about the skirt, and then come back.

I walked to the corner where there was a red light and waited for it to change. As I waited at the curb, other people began surrounding me. Like me, most were tourists. You could tell by their accents, the clothes they were wearing, and the cameras around their necks.

The light was at a busy intersection and cars kept whizzing by. It was taking a while for the light to change, and people were getting impatient. Behind me I could hear grumbling and complaints, as well as jostling. Once or twice, someone bumped into me. I was sure that as soon as the light turned green, everyone was going to race across the street.

As we waited, someone bumped into me again.

Then, seconds later, I felt myself being shoved.

I tried to maintain my balance, but I couldn't.

I began falling off the curb.

Straight into the street.

And into the path of an oncoming car!

They say when you have a brush with death, your life flashes before your eyes. It's true.

As I started to fall into the street, I saw so many different memories. It was like a film on fast-forward. The Christmas when I was seven and got the Easy-Bake oven I had asked for. Meeting Kristine and Simone in kindergarten for the first time. The first date I ever went on. I was thirteen and it was with Matthew Arlington to our school's Valentine's Day dance. The calico kitten my parents gave me for my fourteenth birthday. The day Charlotte came to live with us. She'd looked so alone and scared standing in the foyer of our apartment, but I'd raced to give her a hug so she'd know she wasn't alone and that I was glad she was there.

But then, before I fell into the street, before I was run over, a hand grabbed me and yanked me backward.

It was Logan.

"You need to be more careful," he warned. "The crowds here are out of control. No one is polite. Everyone pushes and shoves."

Logan walked me away from the crowd. "Are you okay?" he asked, his voice filled with concern. "You look really shaken."

My heart was racing and there was a lump of fear in my throat. My entire body was trembling. I felt the exact same way as I had that morning.

I was so lucky Logan had grabbed my arm.

If he hadn't, I wouldn't be standing next to him.

"That's two near misses in one day," I whispered.

"You do seem a little accident-prone."

"That's not funny!" I snapped before bursting into tears.

"Ashley! Ashley, I'm sorry!" he said, his voice filled with panic. "I was trying to make you laugh. Please don't cry." He held a small paper bag out to me. "Look, I brought you a present."

"A present?" I sniffed, glancing at the bag. "What is it?"

He handed it to me. "Why don't you find out?"

I peeked in the bag and saw a seashell bracelet. It was almost identical to the one he had bought me yesterday.

"Simone and Kristine told me what happened to the other one," he said.

"You're so sweet!" I exclaimed as I slid the bracelet onto my wrist.

"It's okay to be upset," he said. "You had a close call."

I wiped away my tears. "I feel like such a baby."

"Maybe I'm the problem."

"What do you mean?"

"Ever since you met me, you've been having

all this bad luck. First the railing on your balcony, then the falling boulder. Now this. Maybe I'm a jinx and causing all this to happen."

I couldn't tell if Logan was serious or if he was kidding around.

"I haven't brought the best luck to other people, either," he said, and I knew he was thinking about last summer and Taylor's disappearance.

"No one knows what happened to Taylor," I said. "You can't feel responsible."

"But I do," he said. "If we hadn't had that fight, maybe things wouldn't have ended the way they did."

"What are you saying?" I asked.

"Taylor was upset when she left my cabin," he said. "She once told me that whenever she was upset, she would go off alone so she could think and clear her head. If we hadn't had that fight, maybe she wouldn't have been alone on the deck. Maybe she would have been inside surrounded by other people or in her cabin."

"Have you been feeling this way all along?" I asked.

"Sometimes," he admitted.

"You can't blame yourself for Taylor's disappearance," I insisted. "You had no idea what was going to happen that night. As for me, you saved my life. That doesn't make you a jinx. That makes you my hero. And you know what?"

"What?"

I placed my hands on the front of Logan's jacket, gently tugging him forward so his face would be close to mine. "A hero deserves a kiss."

And I promptly gave him one.

It was almost eleven when Logan and I returned to the ship. We were walking along an outside deck, gazing at the stars and trying to find the Big Dipper, when I turned to Logan.

"Can I tell you something?"

"Sure."

"You promise not to tell anyone else?"

He made an X over his heart. "Promise."

I stared down at the deck and then I looked back up at him. "I'm afraid."

"Afraid? Of what?"

"I don't know," I whispered. I couldn't put

what I was feeling into words, but I tried. "All these accidents keep happening and they keep happening whenever I'm alone. Can I spend the night with you?" I asked. I felt like a little kid who was afraid to sleep with the lights out because she thought there was a monster under the bed. "I'm not sure if Charlotte will be coming back to our cabin. She hasn't the last two nights and I don't want to spend the night alone."

"So you won't," Logan said. "Go get your stuff and then come down to my cabin. I'll meet you there."

I hurried to my cabin and threw a few toiletries and my nightshirt into a backpack. Before leaving, I left a note for Charlotte so she'd know where I was.

When Logan let me into his cabin, I could see he'd done some quick cleaning up. Clothes and towels were no longer covering the floor, his footwear was neatly lined up, and he'd straightened all his different piles.

"You could have left everything the way it was," I said as I walked inside.

"It needed to get done anyway," he said, looking a little embarrassed that I'd found him out.

I went into the bathroom to get ready for bed, and when I came out Logan was shirtless, wearing a pair of gray sweatpants.

"You can have the bed," he said as he grabbed a pillow. "I'll sleep on the floor."

"I can't make you give up your bed," I argued. "I'll sleep on the floor."

Logan shook his head. "No way."

"Then we'll share the bed."

"It's kind of small," he said.

"That's okay."

"Are you sure?"

"I don't mind if you don't."

He shrugged. "Okay." He hopped into the bed, pressing his back against the wall and holding the sheets out so I could slip in next to him. Once I was in bed, he pulled the sheets over us and snuggled close, wrapping an arm over my waist.

"You comfortable?" he asked.

"Uh-huh."

It *was* a tight fit, but it felt nice having Logan holding me close. I could feel the bare skin of his chest pressing against my back through my thin nightshirt. The heat of his body warmed me.

I turned around on my back so I was facing him.

I didn't say anything, but he knew what I wanted him to do. He slowly lowered his body over mine and pressed me into the mattress, kissing me deeply.

I kissed him back, but I didn't do anything to encourage him to take things further. I knew if I wanted to take the next step with Logan, tonight would be the night to do it, but it didn't feel right. My emotions were all over the place and I didn't want to rush into anything I wasn't ready for. I wanted everything to be perfect my first time.

He broke the kiss. "What are you thinking?"

"I can't tell you."

"We don't have to do anything you're not ready to do," he said.

I nodded slowly. "I know."

I turned back on my side, but I made sure Logan's arm was wrapped around my waist and I placed my arm on top of his. He gave me a gentle hug.

"Sweet dreams," he said.

I woke up the following morning to the sounds of Logan bustling around the cabin. I opened my eyes and saw he was dressed for work.

"What time is it?" I asked with a yawn.

"Seven thirty. Go back to sleep."

I buried my head in the pillow. "Are you going to the masquerade ball tonight?"

"Once I finish my shift. What are you going as?"

"That's for me to know and you to figure out," I said teasingly.

He pouted. "Aren't you even going to give me a hint?"

"Nope. You're going to have to wait until the unmasking at midnight."

"Unless I figure it out before then," he shot back.

I stuck my tongue out at him playfully. "You won't."

"Well, just in case you can't wait until midnight, I'm going as a devil, complete with horns and a pitchfork."

"Oooh, the original bad boy! I love bad boys."

"Do you really?" He leaned over the bed and gave me a kiss. "Then I guess I'll have to show you how bad I can get tonight."

All my fears from the night before were gone. I felt much better after a good night's sleep. I also realized how much Logan meant to me. And how much closer I wanted to get to him.

"We'll see then," I said, deciding at that moment that tonight was going to be the night.

I slept for another hour and then went back to my cabin to shower and change my clothes. After that I headed to the Glamorama, the ship's beauty salon and spa. Simone had raved so much about it that I had made an appointment for a day of beauty for Kristine, Simone, Charlotte, and me. When I got to the salon, I found the three of them in the middle of getting pedicures. Kristine's toes were being painted pink, Simone was getting a French manicure, and Charlotte's toes were being painted red. Kristine and Simone were talking to each other while Charlotte had her nose buried in her SAT study guide.

Charlotte glanced up and when she saw me she reached into the back of her book and waved the note I had left the night before. She didn't say anything but she had a disapproving look on her face. I thought it was a little hypocritical of her to be judging me since she had spent two—maybe even three—nights with Sam. Plus, she didn't know all the facts.

I snatched the note out of her hand and didn't say anything.

"Holding out on us?" Simone asked.

"I'm not holding out," I said.

"Then spill!" Kristine eagerly demanded.

"Nothing happened!" I told them, hoping that would put an end to the discussion.

It didn't.

"You spent the night with a hottie like Logan and *nothing* happened?" Simone asked skeptically. "Do you really expect us to believe that?"

"Believe it." I sat in the empty chair between Kristine and Simone, taking off my sandals. Charlotte was two chairs over from us. It was almost like she was distancing herself from my friends. Of course, there was still tension from yesterday afternoon's scene in the costume shop, so I couldn't blame her. But the point of this day, besides being pampered, was for Charlotte to get to know Simone and Kristine better. She never did stuff like this with us when we were at home, and I was determined to draw her into my circle of friends.

"Charlotte, come sit closer," I urged.

"I'm fine where I am," she said, not looking up from her book as she scribbled with a pencil.

"If nothing happened, then why were you with him?" Simone asked.

"I had a little bit of a scare last night and I didn't want to be alone," I said.

Kristine gasped. "What happened?"

"I almost got hit by a car in Nassau. Luckily, Logan pulled me out of the way in time."

Simone's eyes widened. "Are you okay?"

"Did you get hurt?" Kristine asked.

Simone and Kristine kept asking me questions, wanting to make sure I was fine, but Charlotte didn't. Finally, she looked up from her study guide. "You'd better start being more careful," she said sternly. "Otherwise you're not going to see your sixteenth birthday."

That's all she had to say? I was surprised by how cold and impersonal Charlotte's words were. Why didn't I hear any concern in her voice? Was she mad at me?

Then a thought occurred to me. Could the reason why Charlotte was keeping her distance from me and everyone else be because she was afraid of getting too close? Some people, when they lost someone they loved, pulled away from the rest of the world. They felt it was safer not to get involved. They put up a wall and tried to stay detached because they didn't want to go through that pain and heartache again. Charlotte had lost her mother, the most important person in her life. I couldn't imagine how much that had hurt.

"Don't worry, I will," I promised.

"You should have thanked Logan for rescuing you," Simone said, raising her eyebrows. "If you know what I mean."

I ignored her comment and tried to decide what color nail polish I wanted for my toes.

"What are you doing with your hair tonight?" Kristine asked Simone.

"I'm going to get a blowout. How about you?"

"I think I'm going to get a French braid. I know I'm going as a ballerina, but I don't want to wear it in a bun. I always get headaches when I pull my hair back too tightly." Kristine turned to me. "You're lucky you've got that wig. You don't have to do anything except stick it on your head."

I tried not to smile. I couldn't wait until I revealed myself at the unmasking and they saw I was wearing a different costume.

Simone glanced over at Charlotte, who still wasn't talking to us. "Where's Sam?" she asked.

I shot her a look. I didn't want her stirring up trouble and I got the sense she wanted to.

Charlotte kept her eyes glued on her study guide. "He's playing volleyball."

"On which deck?"

The question made Charlotte close her study guide and stare at Simone. Or, I should say, *glare* at her. "Why?"

Simone shrugged nonchalantly. "I thought I might go cheer him on."

"Why?" Charlotte asked again.

"Guys play better when girls are watching," Simone told Charlotte. "Didn't you know that? They like showing off."

Charlotte got out of her seat. "I'm going for my massage."

"Why did you do that?" I asked Simone once she was gone.

"Relax. I was only messing around with her." Simone picked up a copy of *Cosmo* and started flipping through it. "Don't worry, Poindexter is safe. I'm not going to make a play for him."

"Charlotte doesn't know that."

"Then she's not very smart!" Simone exclaimed. "She's my best friend's sister! I'd never go after her boyfriend."

"Just lay off, okay?" I found myself wanting to be protective of my sister. "Charlotte's under a lot of pressure. She's worried about her SATs and the colleges she's applying to. And she's still dealing with a lot of emotional stuff from when her mom died. The last thing she needs is to think that you're after her boyfriend."

* * *

Once her massage was finished, Charlotte left the beauty salon. She said it was because she wanted to spend more time studying in our cabin, but I think it was because she wanted to keep an eye on Sam. Simone, Kristine, and I spent the rest of the day in the salon being treated like princesses, getting pampered, lotioned, massaged, and buffed. By the time we were finished, we felt like we'd shed our old skins and had shiny new ones. Afterwards, we went to the Diablo Deck and had a quick dinner in a coffee shop designed to look like a 1950s diner, ordering cheeseburgers, fries, and chocolate shakes. Then we headed back to our cabins to get ready for the masquerade.

When I got back to my cabin, Charlotte was waiting for me. She was already dressed in her nun costume and had a sourpuss on her face. I wondered if she'd sucked some lemons to achieve the effect. As soon as I walked through the door, she pounced.

"What's the deal with your friend?" she demanded.

"Who?"

"Simone."

Uh-oh. I knew this conversation was going to happen. It was inevitable.

"I don't like the way she's been coming on to Sam."

"It's only harmless flirting," I explained. "That's Simone's thing."

"Make her stop it."

"I already talked to her but I can't *make* her do anything. In fact, if I tell her it's bothering you, it'll only make her do it more. Just ignore her."

"Are you saying you're not going to help me?" Charlotte threw her hands up in the air. "Why am I not surprised? Simone's more like a sister to you than I am, isn't she? Of course you'd choose her over me! I'm related to you by blood! Doesn't that count? Or would you like to pretend that I don't exist?!"

My mouth dropped open. I was stunned by Charlotte's words. Where was all this coming from?

"I don't know how much more of this I can take!" Charlotte cried. "Between studying for my SATs and feeling seasick all the time, now I have to worry about your friend making a play for my boyfriend?"

Charlotte looked like she was going to fall to pieces. What had brought this on? Insecurity? Too much pressure? I went over to her and sat her down on my bed.

"Charlotte, it's not good for you to be this wound up. You need to relax and have some fun. There's more to life than just studying."

"I'll relax after I take my SATs," she said.

"No, you won't." I knew my sister too well. "After that you'll be obsessing about something else." I took her hand in mine. "Charlotte, Simone isn't interested in Sam. She told me that herself. And even after she did, I still warned her to back off. So, you see, I was looking out for you. You don't have to worry about her. Can you please, please, *please* try to have a good time tonight and for the rest of the cruise? You don't even have to buy me a birthday present. All I want is for you to enjoy yourself. It would mean everything to me."

Charlotte took a deep breath. "I'll try. I

promise I'll try." She gave me a hug. "I'm sorry for what I said."

I hugged her back, but inside I was worried. This was definitely something else I needed to discuss with Daddy once we got home. Charlotte had to let up on herself. If she didn't, the pressure was going to destroy her.

The masquerade ball was taking place in the Crystal Pavilion. It was a huge ballroom, as long and wide as a football field. It had been decorated with colored balloons, streamers, and twinkling white lights. Glittering chandeliers with flame-shaped bulbs and dangling crystals hung from the ceiling every few feet. A live band was against the far wall, playing a jazz medley, and there was a buffet with all sorts of tiny appetizers and finger foods. Waiters in tuxedos circulated with silver trays of champagne poured in tall, thin flutes, and waitresses wearing tiny black cocktail dresses offered an array of tantalizing chocolates and tiny pastries.

There was also an open bar. It didn't look like the bartenders were carding anyone, and

I saw a lot of teenage guys walking away with beers and fruity cocktails for their dates.

I didn't drink at all. Sure, I'd gone to parties where the punch was spiked or bottles of wine were smuggled in, but I didn't touch any of it. First, I didn't like the taste. Second, I knew if I *ever* came home drunk, I'd be in major hot water with my parents. I could slide on some things with them—missing my curfew, forgetting to call home, not pulling my grades up high enough even though I was trying as hard as I could— but drinking was the one thing they would *not* allow.

I walked around the ballroom in my wedding gown, knowing I was unrecognizable. Between my eye mask and the thick veil over my head, my face couldn't be seen. It was hot under all the netting and lace but I could tolerate it.

I felt like I was invisible.

There were so many people and so many different costumes. There were pirates and angels. Cowboys and Indians. Rappers and celebrity look-alikes. Witches, Santa Clauses, elves, and superheroes—guys dressed as Batman,

Superman, or Spider-Man. There were also cartoon characters like Bugs Bunny, Mickey Mouse, and Snoopy.

I started searching for people I knew. I wanted to stand inches away from them and hear what they were talking about.

I saw Simone and Kristine in a corner and walked over to them. I thought Kristine looked very elegant in her ballerina costume, and Simone, naturally, was a hot Wonder Woman. As I walked over, I spotted Molly. I instantly recognized her in my belly dancer costume. She was dancing with three guys and holding a glass in one hand. She seemed a bit wobbly while she was dancing and I wondered if she'd been drinking.

I stood as close as I could to Simone and Kristine, trying to hear their conversation. It was hard, because the ballroom was getting more and more crowded. No surprise, they were checking out guys. I listened for a few minutes and decided to come find them later.

After I left, I started searching for Logan. I was keeping my eyes open for devils, but I didn't see any. I was also trying to find Charlotte and Sam, but I didn't see them, either. I knew Finn was going to be a cat burglar, so as soon as I saw one I headed in the opposite direction. I figured Tabitha wouldn't be too far from Finn, and I had no desire to run into either of them tonight.

I did see Molly again, though. This time she wasn't dancing. It looked like she was yelling at someone, but I couldn't see who it was because she was surrounded by so many people. A hand reached out to touch her, but she pulled back. Then she headed toward the glass doors that led out onto the deck. A few seconds later I saw a devil heading in the same direction. I wondered if it was Logan.

Having spotted him, I didn't want to lose sight of him. I wanted to see if he'd be able to recognize me in my costume.

I began walking through the crowded ballroom, but it was hard to make progress as more and more people kept coming in. I was moving only a few steps at a time and it was sweltering underneath my veil. With so many people packed in the ballroom, it was getting hotter and hotter. I needed some air.

After what seemed like an eternity, I reached the doors that led onto the deck.

As soon as I stepped outside, cool air washed over me, providing relief. The deck was deserted, but I was sure it wouldn't be that way for very long.

There was a swimming pool at the end of the deck and I headed toward it, pulling my wedding veil over the top of my head.

As I got closer to the pool, I saw something in the water.

Something floating.

It looked like . . .

But it couldn't be!

I ripped off my eye mask and blinked.

It was.

There was a body floating facedown in the pool—in a belly dancer costume.

I started running toward the pool, but before I could do anything, another girl screamed. After she screamed, one of the waiters raced past me and jumped into the pool. He reached the floating body and flipped it onto its back, pulling it with him as he swam to the side.

When the body was flipped over, I saw the face of who it was and I gasped.

No! I didn't want to believe it. Even after recognizing the costume . . .

It was Molly!

Chapter 19

*M*olly wasn't moving.

Her body was stiff and her open eyes were staring sightlessly at the night sky.

The waiter who pulled her out of the pool placed her down on the deck and began doing CPR, while the girl who had screamed started yelling for a doctor.

But I knew it was too late.

Nothing could help Molly.

I tore my eyes away, unable to watch anymore.

I'd never known anyone who had died.

How could this have happened? I had seen her walk outside just a short while ago. What had happened between the time she left the ballroom and the time she walked onto the deck?

Drawn by the commotion on deck, people

began pouring out of the ballroom, curious about what was going on. As word started to spread throughout the crowd there were gasps of horror and disbelief. Some women even started crying.

"Ashley! Ashley!" A voice called my name and I turned around. It was Logan. He was dressed in his devil costume, holding a black pitchfork. From head to toe, he was wearing red—pants, long-sleeved shirt, and the cape tied around his neck. The cape hung over his shoulders and reached the back of his knees. His entire face was covered with red makeup. A mustache had been drawn under his nose, as well as a pointy beard on his chin, with a black pencil. He'd slicked back his curly hair with gel so that it was smooth and shiny and there were two curved horns on top of his head. He looked sinister and scary, like he'd come directly from Hell.

"I heard someone drowned in the pool," he said, tearing off his black eye mask. "Do they know who?"

"It was Molly," I whispered.

"Molly?" Logan shook his head in disbelief.

"No. It can't be."

At that moment Kristine, Simone, Charlotte, and Sam raced over. Kristine and Simone threw their arms around me, sobbing.

"Thank God you're okay!" Kristine cried.

"We were so worried!" Simone added.

"*Worried?*" I asked.

"We didn't see you all night so we assumed you were with Logan," Simone said. "But then we heard that someone wearing a belly dancer costume was found dead in the swimming pool."

"As soon as we heard that, we thought it was you!" Kristine sobbed.

"But they were wrong," Charlotte whispered. "They were wrong. You're not dead. You're alive."

Charlotte stared at me like I was a ghost. It was almost as if she couldn't believe I was standing before her.

"Hey! I'm okay," I reassured her, wrapping my arms around her in a hug. Although the circumstances were horrible, this was the first time I felt really close to Charlotte. She *did* care about me. I could see how worried she'd been just by looking at her. She seemed like she was ready to break into pieces. As I tightened my hug, I could feel her trembling.

"I'm okay," I told her again.

"You're really alive," she whispered.

"I switched costumes yesterday with Molly," I explained as I ended my hug with Charlotte. "I wanted to fool everyone."

"What happened?" Simone asked. "Did she fall into the pool?"

"Who said she fell in?" Sam asked, pushing away the black eye patch that covered his right eye. He was dressed as a pirate, complete with a stuffed parrot on his shoulder. "Maybe she was pushed."

When I heard those words from Sam, my blood turned cold.

"Who would want to kill Molly?" Logan asked. "It makes no sense."

"Are you saying there's a killer on board?" Charlotte asked Sam.

"This ship is cursed!" Kristine shouted. "Cursed! Last summer Taylor Morton disappeared into thin air and now Molly has been murdered! What's going to happen next?"

Charlotte, now back in control and always the voice of reason, snapped at Kristine. "Stop being ridiculous! This ship isn't cursed."

Kristine ignored her. "What if Taylor's killer is still on the loose? And what if Molly knew something about Taylor's disappearance?"

"After all this time?" Charlotte asked skeptically. "I don't think so."

"Maybe she remembered something she had forgotten," Kristine stubbornly insisted. "And Taylor's killer saw that she remembered and had to get rid of her. Or maybe she confronted the killer."

"That would be crazy," Simone said.

Confronted the killer . . .

Before heading out onto the deck, Molly had been arguing with someone in the ballroom. When she left the ballroom, she had been followed by someone in a devil costume.

And now she was dead.

But there were probably other devils at the ball. I had no proof that the one following after Molly had been Logan.

And why would Logan want Molly dead?

Unless . . .

Unless he *did* have something to do with Taylor's disappearance last summer and Kristine's theory was right.

We heard that someone wearing a belly dancer costume was found dead in the swimming pool. Simone's and Kristine's words came back to haunt me. *We thought it was you!*

Molly was wearing the costume *I* was supposed to have been wearing.

No one knew I had changed costumes.

What if Molly had been pushed into the pool on purpose and held underwater because the person drowning her thought it was *me*?

But who would want to kill me?

Finn? Could he hate me that much for breaking up with him? If he went home as the guy with the dead girlfriend, everyone would feel sorry for him.

Tabitha? Could she have wanted to get even with me for tossing her in the pool yesterday and decided to get back at me in the same way? If that was true, could things have gone too far?

Logan? That made no sense. Why would Logan want to kill me? We were in love!

Stop it! I scolded myself. *STOP IT!* No one

had plotted to kill me. I couldn't keep thinking like this or I'd drive myself crazy. Molly had drowned. When I saw her dancing earlier, she'd looked wobbly. Maybe she had been drunk and she'd fallen into the pool.

Then I remembered something else and relief flooded through me.

Neither Finn, Tabitha, nor Logan knew I was supposed to be wearing the belly dancer costume. And when Logan asked me what my costume was, I wouldn't tell him!

But . . .

"Where has Sam been all night?" I asked Charlotte pointedly.

"With me," she answered, looking at me with confusion. "Why do you want to know?"

I ignored her question. "The entire night? Are you sure? *Positive?*"

"Yes," she said.

I walked away from Charlotte and searched for Logan. I saw he was talking with a crowd of waiters who he sometimes worked with. As I waited for him to finish, Kristine came over to me.

"I'm so glad you're okay," she said, giving

me another hug. "When we couldn't find you, we panicked. But we figured you were probably with Logan."

"Why would you think that?" I asked. "The ballroom was packed. There was no way Logan could find me, especially since he didn't know what I'd be wearing."

"But he did," Kristine reluctantly admitted.

"What do you mean?" I asked as goose bumps started to rise on my arms and I felt the beginning pinpricks of horror.

I knew what she was going to say before she even said it.

"We ran into him this morning and he asked us to tell him what your costume was," Kristine confessed. "So we told him. He knew what you'd be wearing."

"Are you okay, Ashley?" Simone asked, joining us. "You're so pale."

"I'm fine," I whispered as my mouth turned dry, staring at Logan across the deck as Kristine's words echoed in my mind.

He knew what you'd be wearing. He knew what you'd be wearing. HE KNEW WHAT YOU'D BE WEARING. . . .

I pulled away from Kristine and Simone, running across the deck and trying not to fall in my wedding dress. My legs felt like they were slogging through mud. I could hardly lift them. Was this what it felt like when you were paralyzed by fear? I had to get away. Now! Behind me, I could hear Logan calling my name, but I ignored him.

I ran back to my cabin and locked the door, wishing I could push a pile of furniture in front of it.

By this point, I was trembling, nearly hyperventilating.

I was also wondering, was I on a cruise with a killer?

And was I going to be his next victim?

Chapter 20

Seconds after I locked my cabin door, there was a knock.

The sound made me jump away and I stared at the door in fear.

I knew who it was and I didn't want to answer.

I stood still, holding my breath. I thought if I pretended not to be there, he would go away.

But he didn't.

He knocked again. Harder this time.

"Ashley? Open the door." The doorknob wiggled. "I know you're in there. I saw you go in."

It was Logan.

I slowly walked back toward the door, but I didn't unlock it. "I'm not feeling well, Logan," I said, trying to keep my voice steady.

"Are you sick?"

"I'm really upset."

"We're all upset. You shouldn't be alone."

"I'm fine. Really."

"No, you're not," he insisted. "Otherwise you'd let me in. Come on, Ashley." The doorknob wiggled again. "Open the door."

"Logan, *please*," I pleaded with him. "I can't deal with what happened tonight and I need to be by myself. Try to understand."

"But I want to be there for you. I want to help."

"You'll help if you go away. If you care about me at all, you'll do it."

Logan sighed. "If that's what you want. Fine. I'll see you tomorrow."

I listened to the sound of Logan's retreating footsteps. After he was gone, I threw myself down on my bed and buried my face in my pillow. I wanted to cry, but the tears wouldn't come.

An hour later Charlotte found me still lying on my bed in my costume.

"So this is where you disappeared to. Why are you hiding?"

"I'm not hiding," I said.

"Looks like you're hiding to me," she said, taking off her habit and removing the pins in her hair, shaking the strands free.

"I'm thinking," I told her.

"About what?"

"Molly."

At the sound of her name, Charlotte turned pale. "I still can't believe she's dead. It's so awful. I hope she didn't suffer." She shuddered. "What a horrible way to die."

"Stop it!" I shouted, childishly putting my hands up against my ears. "Stop it! I don't want to hear any more!"

"I'm sorry," Charlotte said, taking a seat on the edge of my bed. "I didn't mean to upset you, but you brought her up. She's dead, Ashley. We can't change that. Sometimes talking about it helps. It helps more than you might know."

"How can it help?" I sobbed, collapsing against Charlotte.

She held me close. "Pretending it didn't happen isn't going to change things. People die every day. That's life. Accidents happen." Charlotte's voice began to quiver. "You never know what's going to happen. My mother died in a car accident. I didn't expect that to happen, but it did and I was devastated. Overnight, my life was changed."

"I'm sorry," I sniffed.

"Don't be sorry," she said. "Just remember that life can take us in unexpected directions. You might think you know what's going to happen next, but you don't. Look at Molly. She's the perfect example. I'm sure when she woke up this morning, she didn't think today was going to be the last day of her life."

Charlotte's words left me speechless. I didn't know what to say back, so I said nothing and went to bed.

When I woke up the following morning, I was officially sixteen.

I was supposed to be feeling happy, but I wasn't. I'd slept horribly the night before, twisting and turning in my bed, suffering from nightmares. Some of my dreams focused on Molly. She was in the pool, reaching out to me, wanting me to save her, but I couldn't get to her in time. My other dreams focused on Taylor.

In those, she was hanging over the side of the ship, trying to keep from falling into the ocean, but her fingers were slipping off the railing. I couldn't save Taylor, either.

Why was I dreaming about two dead girls?

Logan.

They were both connected to him and now they were both dead.

Tonight was my party and it should have been the first thing on my mind when I opened my eyes. I should have been thinking about my hair, makeup, and dress.

But I wasn't.

I was thinking of Molly and Taylor.

They were never going to have another birthday.

I turned my head and saw a bouquet of daisies on the nightstand between my bed and Charlotte's.

"Happy birthday!" she exclaimed, coming out of the bathroom, a towel wrapped around her hair, turban style. "Those are from me. You'll get your real present later tonight at your party."

I sat up in my bed and fingered the petals

of the daisies. "They're so pretty. How did you know daisies are my favorite?" I had never mentioned it before to Charlotte.

"We're sisters," she said. "Sisters are supposed to know those kinds of things." She sat on the side of my bed and put a hand on my knee. "Listen, I'm sorry I wasn't more supportive last night. You needed comforting but I was pretty much still in shock."

"We all were. But you did help. You gave me a reality check," I said, realizing it was true. "Life is short and you never know what's going to happen next."

"Are you excited about your party tonight?" Charlotte asked.

I shook my head. "I think I'm going to cancel my Sweet Sixteen party."

"You can't!" Charlotte exclaimed, sounding alarmed.

"Why not?"

"Think of all the money Dad spent."

That was true. Daddy had rented a private room for my party and it was being decorated according to my specifications, including an ice sculpture. The ship's chef was going to be making all my favorite dishes, as well as my birthday cake, and I was going to have my own d.j. spinning music for me.

"I know, but Daddy would understand. It just doesn't feel right."

"Molly would want you to have your party."

I remembered how excited Molly had been when I had invited her. "I don't know."

Charlotte got off my bed, undoing her turban and using the towel to dry the excess water from her hair. "Discuss it with Simone and Kristine. See what they say. I bet they tell you to still have your party."

Simone and Kristine were waiting for me at breakfast. They'd ordered my favorite, cinnamon French toast with real maple syrup, bacon, and hash browns. It smelled delicious, but I didn't have much of an appetite.

"Happy birthday!" Kristine shouted when she saw me.

"Another year older, another year hotter," Simone added.

They then sang me the "Happy Birthday"

song, much to my embarrassment. I could see a few diners from other tables glancing our way.

I shushed them. "Shhh! Keep it down!"

"So everyone is talking about Molly's drowning," Kristine said as soon as I took my seat.

"Do we have to talk about Molly?" Simone sighed. "It's Ashley's birthday. Can't it wait until tomorrow?"

"What are they saying?" I asked as I picked up a knife and fork and started cutting into my French toast. Even though I wasn't hungry, I knew I had to eat to keep up my strength.

"Molly's death is being considered an accident," Kristine said.

I dipped a piece of French toast into some syrup. "It is?"

Kristine nodded knowingly while adding cream cheese to a bagel. "Just another teenager partying too much."

"A couple of people saw her drinking during the ball," Simone added, taking a sip of orange juice. "Sounds like she was wasted."

"So they think she got drunk, fell into the pool, and drowned?" I asked.

"That's the theory," Kristine said, biting into her bagel.

I hadn't seen Molly as a drinker, but then again, I hadn't really known her. For all I knew, she had a whole other side that I knew nothing about.

"Did you get any prezzies yet?" Kristine asked.

·"Charlotte bought me some daisies. She said I'll get my real present from her tonight."

"That's when you're going to get ours too," Simone said.

"How about Logan?" Kristine asked.

Logan had called the cabin three times that morning before I left, leaving messages since I hadn't picked up the phone. He'd also slipped a note under the door, telling me that he was thinking of me.

· I still hadn't called him back.

"I haven't gotten anything from Logan yet," I said.

"I bet he surprises you at your party tonight," Kristine said.

"About my party . . ." I started to say.

"Have you convinced her not to cancel her

birthday party?" Charlotte asked, coming up to the table.

Charlotte was wearing a cute white tennis skirt and matching polo top, holding a tennis racquet in one hand. Standing behind her in his tennis whites and holding a racquet of his own was Sam.

"Cancel your party?" Kristine asked. "Why would you want to do that?"

I shrugged. "With everything that's happened, it doesn't feel right to me."

"You only turn sixteen once," Simone reminded me.

"If it makes you feel better, we can have a moment where we all talk about Molly," Charlotte suggested. "We all knew her. Would that make you feel better?"

"I think that would be nice," Kristine said.

"And we were all looking forward to your party," Simone said. "Weren't you? How can you cancel it?"

I threw up my hands in surrender. "Okay, okay! We'll have the party."

"Yay!" Charlotte exclaimed. "I'm so glad the party is still on! Mark my words, Ashley.

Tonight is going to be a night you never forget!"

Logan tracked me down after breakfast as I was heading back to my cabin. I had been planning to hide out from him there for the rest of the morning.

"What's going on?" he asked, cornering me in a hallway.

"What do you mean?"

"You disappeared on me last night and you haven't returned my phone calls," he said. "Something is up."

I couldn't avoid it any longer.

"Where were you all last night?" I hated asking the question; I hated doubting him, but I needed to know. "I was looking all over for you."

"I was stuck working a double shift. I got to the ball a couple of minutes before Molly was found."

Was he telling the truth? I wondered. Or was he lying? How easy would it be to slip away, shove Molly into the pool, and then return to the ball?

I stared into Logan's gray eyes, expecting to see the cold, ruthless eyes of a killer. Instead, I saw nothing but warmth, love, and concern. He wasn't a killer. He couldn't be.

"You didn't see Molly at all last night?"

Logan looked at me with confusion. "What's with all the questions about Molly? I just told you I had to work a double shift. What are you thinking?"

"Because I saw someone who I thought was you following Molly out onto the deck," I explained.

"How do you know it was me?" Logan asked. "Everyone was in costume. It could have been someone else."

"Yes, it could have been," I admitted.

"But you don't believe me."

"Of course I believe you."

Maybe I didn't say it fast enough. Maybe I hesitated for a second. Or maybe there was something in the way I said the words. But Logan stared at me in shock.

"You think I had something to do with Molly's death, don't you?"

"I never said that!" I cried.

"You don't have to. It's written all over your face."

Logan walked away and I hurried after him.

Why had I even said anything?

I didn't even know what I saw!

I didn't know if Molly had argued with Logan.

And I didn't know if Logan was the one who had followed her out onto the deck.

I didn't even know if Molly had been murdered. Her death could have been a tragic accident the way everyone was saying.

I caught up with Logan and touched him on the arm but he shook me off.

"Everything you told me last night was a lie, wasn't it?" he hissed. "You weren't upset. You didn't need to be alone. You were afraid of me!"

I felt awful about what had just happened. Awful! And I didn't know how to fix it. Was it even fixable?

"I didn't know what I was doing last night," I explained, hoping he would understand. "Yes,

I was scared, but I was also confused. I still am! So many strange things have been happening on this cruise."

"Well, let me help you with your confusion," Logan said, staring at me. "I won't be showing up at your birthday party tonight. In fact, you never have to worry about seeing me again."

When I stared back into Logan's eyes, all the warmth, love, and concern were gone.

Now his eyes were cold and empty.

I spent the rest of the day trying not to think of Logan. I didn't tell anyone about our fight. How could I? If I said anything, I would make Logan look guilty and cause a lot of trouble for him. He could be questioned about Molly's drowning. He could even lose his job. After all, he'd been questioned last year when Taylor had disappeared. It would look bad for the cruise line to have an employee considered a suspect in two tragedies, even if he was cleared both times. And I hadn't seen anything! I couldn't prove anything! All I had were my suspicions and I was doubting them.

Kristine and Simone spent the day with me. We played Ping-Pong and shuffleboard, took a Pilates class, went to another fashion show, and window-shopped in the ship's jewelry store, admiring all the gorgeous rings, bracelets, and necklaces that we couldn't afford. We went for a swim in the pool and tanned ourselves for a little bit, having lunch poolside. Again, it was my favorites: chicken salad, onion rings, and cupcakes for dessert. Then we went to the ship's karaoke bar and sang a bunch of different songs (Simone, the diva, kept selecting Jennifer Lopez songs for herself, while Kristine and I stuck with duets). I always made sure I was smiling so they wouldn't know anything was wrong. I was afraid if they started asking questions, I would spill and tell them everything.

I just wanted this day over with.

I wanted this entire cruise over with.

All I wanted was to go home where I felt safe.

Where there weren't any accidents or deaths.

When it was finally time to get ready for

my party, Kristine and Simone went off to their cabin and I went to mine. Charlotte was already gone when I arrived, so I had the whole cabin to myself.

Since my birthday dress had been slashed, I decided to wear one of the dresses I had brought along. I went with a strapless buttercup-yellow silk chiffon and I matched it with a pair of yellow slides that had bows on the front. I left my hair down but held it off my face with two hair combs decorated with tiny yellow roses. I knew the sharp metal tines of the combs would be digging into my scalp by the end of the night — they always did — but I liked how pretty they were. They'd been a gift from my grandparents on my last birthday, so I was sentimental about them. When it came to makeup, I plumped up my lashes with some mascara and added a touch of smoky eye shadow to my lids. I decided not to wear any lipstick but went with some lip gloss so my lips were shiny and wet. Jewelry was very minimal. Just a gold necklace around my neck. I finished by giving myself a spritz of perfume.

As I got ready, I couldn't stop thinking of Logan. He'd looked so betrayed after our last conversation! How could I have said the things I did? I had to find him and apologize before my party. I had to explain to him again how scared I had been last night and how I hadn't been thinking clearly. Deep down, I knew he hadn't had anything to do with Molly's drowning. I only hoped he would forgive me and give me a second chance.

Before leaving the cabin, I took a final look in the mirror and liked what I saw. Part of me hoped Logan would too. At the last minute, I decided to wear the bracelet he had given me. I hoped he'd notice.

When I opened the door, I was surprised to find a long white box outside. It looked like the kind of box that would hold long-stem roses.

I picked up the box excitedly and brought it inside, removing the red ribbon wrapped around it. Who could have sent me roses?

I lifted off the top of the box and pushed aside the mounds of white tissue paper, eager to uncover the roses.

But what was inside the box wasn't quite what I had expected to find.

The box was filled with a dead rose bouquet. The once bright red petals were black and curling. The green leaves were crisp and crumbling and the stems were dry and brittle.

The entire bouquet was wrapped with a black silk ribbon and nestled against the bouquet was a note.

GET READY FOR A NIGHT YOU'RE NEVER GOING TO FORGET.

The note was signed: *LOGAN.*

Chapter 21

I backed away from the box in horror.

A scream started building in my throat, but I wouldn't let it out.

How could Logan have sent me something so awful? Did he hate me that much?

And what was he planning next? An accident like Molly's? A disappearance like Taylor's?

Clearly, he had gone off the deep end.

And now my life was in danger.

Why hadn't I told anyone what I saw or what I suspected?

I needed to go to the ship's captain and tell him everything. I should have done it last night. But I hadn't wanted to believe Logan was guilty.

I shuddered as I stared at the box, not wanting to be alone anymore. I wanted to be surrounded by my friends. I'd get them to come with me to see the captain.

I ran to the phone and called Simone and Kristine's cabin. The line kept ringing and ringing.

"Come on! Answer!" I begged before hanging up when the voice mail message came on.

I tried Sam's cabin next, hoping he and Charlotte might be there. No answer. I even called Finn's cabin, and Tabitha's.

No one was around.

Where were they?

I had never before felt so scared and alone. It was like I was the last person on the planet.

Then I realized where they were. At my birthday party. That's why I couldn't reach any of them. Now that I knew where they were, I wanted to be with them. They would all protect me from Logan.

Who knew what he would try to do to me?

When I arrived at the ballroom where my party was to take place, all the lights were turned off. I suspected that everyone was hiding in the dark, waiting to jump out and yell happy birthday.

As I walked deeper into the room, I waited for the lights to go on.

I waited to see everyone with smiles on their faces.

But the lights remained off. No one yelled happy birthday.

I began searching for a light switch, feeling against the wall. Could I be the first one to arrive? But I was never the first one to arrive anywhere on time.

I began to feel uneasy.

Something was wrong, very wrong. I could feel it.

I began to retrace my steps. As I did, I found the light switch. With a sigh of relief, I flipped it up.

I expected to see the room decorated like an English garden, with flowers draped everywhere. There were supposed to be white balloons and white streamers along the ceiling and a wishing well ice sculpture where pennies could be tossed in.

But the entire room was trashed.

Flowers were thrown everywhere, smashed on the floor, and dirt from the planters had been flung at the walls. Balloons had been popped and streamers were torn. The ice sculpture was tipped over and cracked, melting into a puddle. Dishes and glasses were broken and the padded backs of the chairs surrounding the dinner table had been slashed, the stuffing pulled out.

As I stared at the destruction, all I saw was rage.

It looked like a crazy person had attacked everything.

Crazy person . . .

Logan!

I whirled around, almost expecting to find him behind me, but no one was there.

I raced back to the door I'd come in through, but when I went to open it, it was locked.

I pounded against it.

"Hey! Let me out!" I shouted, trying to stay calm. Trying not to panic. "Let me out! Somebody help me!"

And then the room plunged back into darkness.

I turned around, pressing my back against the door, my heart pounding furiously inside my chest. It was pounding so hard, I thought it was going to break free.

Had the lights gone out on their own? Or had someone turned them off?

If someone had turned them off, then that meant I wasn't alone.

I choked back a sob and tried to get a grip on myself. I couldn't lose it! If I wanted to get out of there alive, I needed to have a clear head.

I stood still, deciding to remain in place. As long as I stayed here, I'd be safe. Logan couldn't attack me from behind.

But then I heard something.

Something that made my skin crawl.

The sound of breathing.

It was getting closer.

And closer.

I was afraid! More afraid than I'd ever been in my entire life.

I started kicking against the locked door with the back of my feet. "Help me!" I screamed. "Somebody please help me!"

Was there another way out of the room? I wondered. If there was, how could I find it?

Then, as I stared into the darkness, I saw something at the end of the room.

A flicker of light.

It began coming closer.

And closer.

Then I heard singing.

The sounds of "Happy Birthday."

The light was coming from candles on a birthday cake.

As the light came closer, I could see it was Charlotte holding the cake.

At the sight of my sister, I felt relief. Had this all been a setup? Were they all punking me? "You don't know how scared I was!" I exclaimed, laughing nervously.

But then I noticed something.

The birthday cake that Charlotte was holding.

It was smashed.

"Time to make a wish before you die," Charlotte whispered as she gave me a smile that was pure evil.

Chapter 22

*Y*ou?" I gasped.

Not Finn.

Not Tabitha.

Not Sam.

Not Logan.

Charlotte! It had been Charlotte the entire time.

"That's right, little sister," she said, the light of the birthday candles casting eerie shadows over her face. "It's been me."

"But why?" I couldn't understand it. It didn't make any sense! "Why would you do all those horrible things?"

Charlotte put down the cake and reached into her skirt pocket for a remote control. She aimed it at the wall and returned it to her pocket as the lights came back on.

I thought the darkness going away would make me feel less afraid, but it didn't.

It made me even more afraid.

In the light, Charlotte's rage was fully exposed. It was written all over her face. And it was aimed directly at me.

"Easy," she said. "I hate you."

I couldn't believe what I was hearing. I had been nothing but kind to Charlotte since she came to live with us. Her words were like a knife plunging into my heart. "You *hate* me?"

"Ever since I was a little girl, I've hated you," she revealed, her voice rising. "You're the one who always had our father. You're the one who always had everything handed to you on a silver platter. What have I had?" she screamed. "Nothing!"

"That's not true," I told her. "You had your mother."

"My mother," she whispered, her face crumbling for a second before turning hard again. "Don't you dare *mention* my mother! Do you know how my mother died, Ashley?"

Why was she asking me this question? "It

was a car accident."

"She was driving back home from a bakery with a birthday cake. She hadn't spent my sixteenth birthday with me because she had to work, so we were going to celebrate that night. Did you know that?"

I shook my head. I don't think any of us did. And Charlotte had never told us.

"I couldn't have a Sweet Sixteen party because we didn't have enough money. All she could afford was a cake. I really didn't care about having a party. Some of my friends had taken me out for lunch the weekend before and they'd given me presents. I knew how hard my mom worked to support us and how special she wanted to make things, so spending my birthday with her meant a lot to me. But we never celebrated my birthday or had that cake because she was hit by another car. There was no over-the-top birthday cruise for *me*," Charlotte raged. "No extravagant allowance or shopping sprees!"

"But you have all that now," I told her, even though I knew it could never replace her mother. "And don't you remember what I told you the other day? When you graduate from high school, Daddy is going to send you to any college you want. You're also going to get a trust fund, did you know that? Daddy set one up for both of us. You'll be able to spend the money on whatever you want."

Charlotte laughed in my face. "You don't get it, do you? Do you think I really care about all this *stuff*? About money and things? If you do, you're even stupider than I thought!" she sneered. "None of that matters to me! All I had was my mother. And then when I lost her, I was sent to live with you. I got to see what you always had and it made me hate you even more. All I ever really wanted was a family. But I never had that. *You* had that your entire life."

"But you have that now," I reminded her, scrambling to find the right words to calm Charlotte down. "Isn't that what you've always wanted?"

I needed Charlotte to see how much she would lose if she continued with this twisted plan of hers. I didn't know what was going to happen next, but I had to stop her from whatever else she was going to do.

"It's not the same!" Charlotte screamed. "It's *yours*! It's *always* been yours and not mine!"

"Maybe that's true," I said slowly. "But now it's *ours*. It's *our* family."

"Shut up!" she screamed, covering her ears. "Shut up! Shut up! Shut up! I don't want to hear any of it. You're lying. You'll say anything to save yourself."

"Charlotte, you don't want to do this." I looked around the room, trying to find another way out. I searched for a second door, but I didn't see one. There was just the one door I had come through. How had Charlotte locked it when she had been hiding at the other end of the room?

Then I remembered the remote control in her pocket. She must have used it to lock the ballroom door the same way she had turned the lights on and off. I had to get it away from her. It was my only chance of escaping.

"Yes, I do," she said, a satisfied smile

washing over her face. "I've been planning this for months."

"Planning what?" I asked, afraid of her answer.

Charlotte giggled and chills traveled down my spine.

"Your birthday murder."

I stared at her in shock. I couldn't have heard her right.

"Charlotte, you don't want to kill me." I began frantically searching the room with my eyes for something, *anything*, I could use to defend myself.

She shrugged. "Why not? I've killed before."

"Y-Y-You've killed before?" I gasped in disbelief.

Charlotte's eyes gleamed with insanity as she nodded.

I could barely get my next question out. "Wh-wh-who?"

"I'll give you a clue," she giggled. "She was wearing your belly dancer costume."

"You murdered Molly?" I asked.

"That's right," Charlotte said. "She didn't

fall into the pool. I pushed her in and I held her head under the water too. At first she fought me but eventually she gave up. She'd been drinking and she didn't have much strength to fight me." Charlotte glared at me. "But she wasn't the one who was supposed to die last night. It was supposed to be *you*! I thought *you* were the one I was drowning!"

Hearing Charlotte's words, I almost fainted. But I didn't. I couldn't. I had to keep thinking. I had to figure out a way to save myself.

"It's your fault she's dead, you know," Charlotte continued.

"*My* fault?" I gasped.

Charlotte angrily nodded. "If you hadn't switched costumes with her, I wouldn't have killed her by mistake. Imagine how shocked I was when I came out by the pool and saw you standing there. I expected to find *you* floating in the water, not her."

I remembered Charlotte's behavior the night before. Her pale face. Her trembling body. She had been in shock because she had realized her mistake of killing the wrong girl. Everything she had said now had new meaning. She had stared at me with disbelief and couldn't believe I was alive because she thought she had killed me. She hadn't been concerned about me at all.

"It's not my fault Molly is dead. It's yours!" I shouted. "*You* killed her. Not me."

"I didn't mean to kill her. It was an accident. Don't think I don't feel bad. I do. Molly never did anything to me." Charlotte shrugged. "She was in the wrong place at the wrong time."

I stared at my sister like she was a stranger. I really didn't know anything about her. I never had. All this time, she'd hated me and I didn't know. She'd done such a good job of disguising her true feelings.

"You never even suspected me, did you?" she asked, as if reading my mind. "You had no clue how much I hated you. You were off in your own little world, with your parties and shopping and boyfriends. With a mother and father who loved you and gave you everything you ever wanted." Charlotte's face twisted with hatred, "All I ever got from our father were the scraps that he tossed to me. You were his precious, precious Ashley and I was his forgotten daughter. Sometimes I hate him as much as I hate you," she hissed. "But that's wrong. A daughter isn't supposed to hate her father. She's supposed to love him, right?"

I nodded slowly, wondering what she was going to say next.

"But how could I love him when he gave you all his love? There was never any for me. And then I realized that if you weren't around, *I'd* be his only daughter. *I'd* get all his love and attention because he'd only have me." Charlotte laughed cruelly. "But then I'd leave him the way he left me when I was a little girl and he'd have no one to love him. He'd be all alone! He'd know what it felt like for me all those years ago. After I realized that, I started planning."

The words slipped out before I could stop them. I don't know why I said them. Maybe it was because I didn't want Charlotte to think she was as smart as she thought she was. "He wouldn't be alone. He'd have my mother."

Charlotte smirked. "Would he?"

My body went numb. "What do you mean?"

"Didn't I tell you?"

"Tell me what?"

"I'm afraid your mother is going to have a little *accident* after she hears about your death," Charlotte said matter-of-factly. "Poor Daddy. Losing both his wife and daughter in such a short period of time. But don't worry, I'll be there for him. That is, until I leave for college and never come back. So you see, Ashley, our father *will* be alone. I'm going to make sure of that."

I was paralyzed with fear. Charlotte was crazier than I thought. I had to stop her. My life wasn't the only one at stake.

Charlotte laughed again. "Why do you think I was so eager to help you with this birthday cruise? Why do you think I even suggested a cruise to the Bahamas? I wanted us to come on *this* ship."

"You did. But why?"

"Taylor Morton," Charlotte explained. "She mysteriously disappeared on this ship last year. I read all about it. I decided *you* would mysteriously disappear too. The authorities would think that whatever had happened to Taylor had happened to you. No one would even suspect me! It was going to be the perfect murder."

I had to keep her talking. I peeked over my shoulder at the locked door. Eventually someone would show up for my party. Kristine. Simone. I'd even take Sam, Finn, or Tabitha!

"You tried to kill me before last night, didn't you?"

Charlotte laughed. "It was so much fun scaring you! *I* was the one behind everything. *I* loosened the balcony railing. *I* locked you in the sauna. *I* tampered with those shoes, knowing you'd eventually borrow them! So selfish! I hadn't even worn them but *you* had to wear them first. You fell right into my trap. Into all my traps! *I* was the one who left that message in lipstick and called you in the middle of the night. What I really enjoyed was slashing your precious birthday dress. Do you know why?"

I couldn't answer.

"As I was slashing the fabric, I pretended the knife was slashing through your flesh, cutting it to ribbons," she hissed.

"You're the one who pushed that boulder?" I asked, even though I knew it was true. "Who shoved me in front of that car?"

"You were supposed to die those times, but you didn't!" Charlotte screamed, her face twisting with hatred. "Your death was supposed to look like an accident! Even though I wanted to push you overboard like Taylor, even though that was my original plan, I couldn't wait." She noticed me peeking over my shoulder again at the closed door. A satisfied smile appeared on her face—like she knew something I didn't— and it made my skin crawl.

"No one's coming," she whispered.

"What?" I croaked, not wanting to believe her.

"You keep looking at the door. You think someone's going to come to your rescue. Well, guess what? They're not. Want to know why?"

I swallowed over the lump in my throat.

"Why?"

"I changed the time of the party. Everyone is going to be here an hour from now. And when they arrive, they're going to find you dead. Along with your killer by your side."

"My killer?"

"Someone has to take the blame."

Charlotte walked over to a closet against the wall and opened the door. Logan's unconscious body fell out.

I ran over to his side. "What have you done to him?" I cried, frantically searching for a pulse, a breath, some sign that he was still alive! Logan couldn't be dead. He couldn't!

"Calm down!" Charlotte snapped. "I slipped a sedative into the soda I gave him. Good old Bishop Pharmaceuticals! They have everything you need when planning a murder!" she laughed. "Logan was the icing on the cake. I couldn't have planned that better myself."

"What do you mean?"

"Blabbermouth Molly told me that Logan had been involved with Taylor last summer. Of course, I already knew that from the articles I had read, but I played dumb. When I saw you were dating him, I knew I could use him in my plan. Frame him. It was too perfect! I lured him down here by telling him I wanted to help patch things up between the two of you." She laughed again. "He thought I was looking out for my baby sister! Did you like the roses I sent? I thought those were a nice touch. More evidence against him!"

My head was spinning. She had thought of everything. And if I didn't find a way to stop her, she was going to get away with it.

Logan would be blamed. Not only would they think that he had killed me, but he would be blamed for Molly's and Taylor's deaths, too. Charlotte would make sure of that.

And then she would go after my mother.

I couldn't let any of that happen. I couldn't.

How could I have ever suspected Logan of all the horrible things Charlotte had done? I felt like such a fool! I should have trusted my heart!

"You don't want to do this," I said, rising to my feet and trying to reason with Charlotte. "We're sisters. You still love me. I know you do." I started to approach her cautiously. I needed to get that remote control out of her pocket! "Let me help you, Charlotte. Before it's too late. I love you."

It was the wrong thing to say. Hearing my

words, Charlotte's face turned ugly and she lunged at me. She caught me off guard and I fell to the floor.

"I hate you!" she screamed as she jumped on top of me. "I hate you!"

Then she wrapped her hands tightly around my throat and started to squeeze.

Chapter 23

I couldn't breathe.

I tried to pry Charlotte's fingers from around my throat, but I couldn't.

My vision became hazy.

I started blacking out.

And then I remembered.

My hair combs!

I reached to the top of my head and pulled one out.

Then I jabbed Charlotte in the face as hard as I could, sinking the metal tines into her skin.

She screamed, releasing her hold.

I broke free of her grasp, struggling for air.

I jumped back to my feet and ran for the phone to dial the ship's security. But before I could press any numbers, Charlotte was behind me, yanking the phone out of the wall.

She had a hand pressed to her bleeding cheek. "You're going to regret doing that, little sister."

I tried to run away from her, but I was too slow. She lunged at me from behind and I fell to the floor with her on my back.

"This time I'm going to finish what I started," she vowed, yanking the other hair comb out of my hair and tossing it to one side.

I fought against Charlotte, trying to throw her off me, but I couldn't. She was too heavy.

And then I saw it.

Part of the melted ice sculpture.

I picked up a chunk of ice about the size of a small club.

When Charlotte flipped me onto my back, I swung the chunk of ice with all my might, hitting her on the side of the head.

Instantly, she collapsed.

I pushed her off me and scrambled inside her skirt pocket for the remote control. As soon as I found it, I aimed it at the ballroom door and ran for it. When I reached the door, I flung it open, screaming for help.

It was finally over.

* * *

Hours later I was alone in my cabin when there was a knock on the door. I opened it, expecting to find Simone and Kristine waiting. They were going to spend the night with me and had gone back to their cabin to get their things. They had shown up for my party just as Charlotte was being taken away in handcuffs. Both had been speechless when I told them what had happened.

Meanwhile, Logan had regained consciousness. He had insisted he was fine, but he was taken to the ship's infirmary to be checked out. We hadn't had a chance to talk.

Now he was standing in front of me.

"How are you doing?" he asked.

"Shouldn't I be asking you that question?"

"I'm fine," he said.

I sighed. "I've been better."

"It's been a rough couple of days."

The words rushed out of my mouth. I had to say them because they were tearing me up inside. "Logan, I'm sorry. I'm so, so sorry! I don't know what else to say. I know it doesn't make up for doubting you and thinking you were responsible for Molly's death and all those horrible things that Charlotte did, but I want you to know—"

Logan pressed a finger to my lips, shushing me.

"It's not your fault. Charlotte was playing head games with you. She fooled all of us."

I noticed Logan's other arm was hidden behind his back. "What are you hiding?" I asked.

He held out a chocolate-frosted cupcake with a lit candle.

"Chocolate's your favorite, right?"

I nodded.

"It's still your birthday," he said. "Make a wish."

I blew out the candle.

"What did you wish for?"

"If I tell you, it won't come true," I whispered.

Logan gave me a smile. "I think I know what you're hoping for."

"You do?"

He nodded, bending his head to mine and giving me a kiss.

It was the sweetest kiss anyone had ever given me.

"Was I right?" he asked.

"You were right," I said softly.

"How about another one?"

Before I could answer, Logan kissed me again.

Epilogue

*I*t's been six months since my birthday cruise.

A lot has happened.

Charlotte is in a mental institution getting the help she needs. No one knew she was unstable. Her doctors also think the combination of all the different pills she was taking might have had something to do with her behavior. Some of the medications were prescribed, but others weren't. Charlotte had been self-medicating herself, going to Daddy's office and helping herself to various samples that were available to the Bishop Pharmaceutical sales reps.

I haven't seen Charlotte since she was taken away in handcuffs. The doctors think it's too soon.

I don't hate my sister. I know, now *I* sound like the crazy one. Yes, she tried to kill me, but she's sick and she needs help. She put so much pressure on herself, studying all the time and trying to be perfect, as well as thinking that no one loved her. Just being herself would have been enough. If only she'd given my parents and me a chance when she'd come to live with us, maybe none of this would have happened.

And even though she did kill Molly, Charlotte inadvertently saved my life. I couldn't forget that.

Because, like Charlotte, *Molly* was also planning to kill me.

Let me backtrack a little.

While we were still on the cruise, the mystery of Taylor Morton's disappearance was solved.

Taylor had been murdered by Molly.

After Molly's death, her cabin was cleaned out. Discovered among her things was her diary. When the police read through it, they discovered that Molly had been obsessed with Logan. She'd been madly in love with him and had been devastated when he started dating Taylor.

When Taylor broke up with Logan,

Molly decided to punish her by pushing her overboard.

Later in the diary, there were entries about me. About how much Molly hated me because I had "stolen" Logan away from her and how she was going to "punish" me the same way she had punished Taylor. With Taylor out of the way, Molly thought she'd have a chance with Logan this summer. Even though Logan only saw Molly as a friend, she thought it was just a matter of time before he changed his mind. But before that could happen, I had come on board the ship and Logan had started going out with me, ruining all of Molly's plans.

So I had to be eliminated.

If Charlotte hadn't drowned Molly, who knows what Molly would have done to me?

The news was hard on Logan when he found out. He blamed himself, not only for Taylor's death, but also for what could have happened to me.

But I was there to help him through it, telling him that none of it was his fault.

We've been dating now that we're back in

New York, and Logan is the best boyfriend I've ever had.

As for everyone else, here's an update.

Finn and Tabitha are no longer a couple. They broke up after the cruise on national TV. Tabitha had invited Finn over for what he thought was a romantic dinner. Instead, she dumped him on MTV's latest reality show, *Dumped!*, telling him that he didn't know how to commit. Finn was outraged, until the show aired and he started getting letters and e-mails from girls wanting to go out with him. Tabitha, meanwhile, is getting her own reality show on MTV called *The Girl Everyone Loves to Hate*. Just so you know, I won't be making a guest appearance on it.

Sam and I are now friends. Charlotte's brought us together. It turns out there was a reason why Sam was always watching me and staring at me. Often, when they were alone, Charlotte would say mean and horrible things about me. She'd rant and rave about how selfish I was, and Sam couldn't understand it because whenever he saw me, I was always so nice to both him and Charlotte. I was a puzzle he was trying to figure out. He never saw the side of me that Charlotte had described, and it left him confused and perplexed.

He also blamed himself for Charlotte's condition. He knew she had been taking so many pills, but he never questioned it. Other times on the cruise she would disappear, and when he asked her where she had been, she wouldn't tell him. Those were probably the times when she was carrying out her plan against me. He felt maybe if he had said something to someone, things wouldn't have gotten so out of control. I told Sam he couldn't think that way. Charlotte's hatred of me had started long before the killer cruise.

Kristine is still Kristine. Sweet, funny, and melodramatic. Simone *finally* found a new boyfriend when classes started again in September. He's a transfer student from London who's got this great British accent. All the girls in our class are jealous, which is just how Simone likes it. Hopefully, they'll still be dating by Valentine's Day. I know Logan and I will be.

So, you see, good things *definitely* come to those who wait! Eventually, the killer cruise docks, and life makes up for any nightmares you've had along the way.

Want more summer romance
with a deadly twist?

Turn the page for an excerpt of

by
TERRI CLARK

"WHEN ARE YOU going to hook up with a hottie?"

I spat out a gulp of Mocha Frappuccino in a movie-worthy spit take and gave my best friend, Coral, a censuring glare. She merely laughed and arched an insistent "answer me" eyebrow.

"Sheesh, Coral," I whined, wiping mocha off my bare legs. "Give a girl some warning before you ax her with a question like that."

She took an exaggerated slurp of iced green tea before saying, "Not a chance, Trinity. You're too smooth at avoidance and misdirection, so I have to catch you off guard. Besides"—she pointed to a spot of melting frap that I'd missed on my bare stomach—"the look on your face was priceless. I only wish I'd caught it on camera."

I rolled my eyes, just imagining her posting my blooper on YouTube. Like people didn't think I was enough of a freak already. Feeling dry, but sticky, I settled back into my lounge chair. We were chillin' out on SoBe in our new bikinis, mine a ruby red with crossbones, hers bubble-gum pink with lime-green polka dots. No doubt we looked luscious, but you couldn't call us your average sun worshippers. Not when we were reclining under an oversized umbrella to protect our skin. Me, because I don't do tan, and Coral, because her fair, freckled skin burns from the slightest rays.

I dug a hole in the sand and tucked my drink into it, then rooted around in my tattoo sling bag for my bottle of Midnight Marauder nail polish. Lavishing my toes with attention, I painted them black and avoided Coral's persistent gaze. "What do you expect me to do?" I asked her. "Pounce on the first guy who walks by?"

Coral gave an inelegant snort, stifling any follow-ups with her hand. I looked up to see what had caused her reaction and shuddered as a fleshy man in a too-tight Speedo strutted by with an impressive amount of confidence— no doubt, a Florida tourist. When we caught sight of his back we both squealed, "Ew!" simultaneously and collapsed onto each other in a fit of giggles. He glowered at us.

"Poor man," Coral whispered, once she regained her composure. "He really should get lasered."

"Imagine the smell of burnt hair," I said and twitched my nose.

"Ack, stop." She puffed out her cheeks like she had to vomit. "Now I'm twice as traumatized."

I grinned and wiggled my nearly dry toes, but just as I let my guard down she swooped in again.

"I'm not letting up on you." She swung her legs over the side of her chair, facing me. Her eyes were alight with her usual energy and exuberance. Admittedly, I loved her contagious enthusiasm, but not when she meant to back me into a corner.

I gave her my typical "here we go again" groan.

She responded by slapping my leg.

"Hey!"

"This is our last summer before college," she said, ignoring my yelp. "We're supposed to live it up! Expand our personal boundaries. Be adventurous. Discover who we are."

She outstretched her arms and I held up a warning finger. "If you start singing 'Breaking Free,' there's going to be bloodshed."

Coral smirked. "Apropos—but I was going for 'Unwritten.'"

"A better choice," I conceded. Lord knows I'd take Natasha Bedingfield over *High School Musical* any day. "But save the solo. I get your point. Summer equals freedom."

"No!" Coral shouted. "It's more than that. Here it is, July seventh, and classes start on August twenty-seventh. It's going fast! This should be a summer of change. Of metamorphosis. Of transmogrification."

"Great, now you're going all Harry Potter on me," I mumbled. "I'm not morphing into a cat."

"That's not what I meant. We"—she waved a finger between the two of us—"can be whoever we want. We're not tied to the labels we were given in high school."

"You mean Goth Girl and Soccer Star?" I shot a glance from my piratical swimsuit to the soccer ball under her chair. "Gee, so much has changed," I sneered.

Coral blew out an exasperated breath. "I don't mean that. Will you listen?"

I folded my arms over my chest and locked

my gaze on her. "Undivided attention."

"Thank you," she said. "I'm not talking about the core things that make us . . . well, us. Yes, you're Goth Girl and I'm Soccer Star, but we're more than that."

"Here it comes," I interrupted and then bit my lip when she motioned for me to zip my mouth.

"I'm klutzy and clueless," she admitted.

"You're comical and naïve," I defended.

She pointed to a bevy of bruises on her legs. "Connect the dots, babe," she told me.

"Fine," I said, "so you're klutzy. It's part of your charm."

She smiled at me, grasping my hand. "I know you love me just the way I am, Trin. You're my best friend. But I *would* like to be a little more poised and I hate feeling like I'm always missing the punch line." She let go of me and shrugged. "I've always been too sheltered and you"—she gave me a sad smile, not a piteous one, but a compassionate one—"you've seen too much."

I opened my mouth to object, thinking she wasn't nearly as naïve as she believed, but she spoke before I could.

"There's a part of you I don't even know," she said softly.

I lowered my eyes, unable to deny it. Still, after all these years, unable to explain.

"It's okay," she said. "I know enough about you to be sure of one thing. You take too much of the world on your shoulders and you don't allow yourself to be."

Be? It sounded like such a simple word.

"You hold back, Trin. You hide. I don't know why, but you're like a turtle. Your shell protects you and keeps you hidden. When are you going to peek your head out?"

When indeed? I didn't know how to answer, couldn't . . .

Being the smart chick she is, Coral quickly realized her point had hit home and she snapped back to her bubbly self so as not to push me too far. "You know what we're going to do this summer?"

"Uh"—I scrunched up my face as if in heavy concentration—"you're going to soccer camp and I'm going to wallow in loneliness?"

"You're only half right," she chirped.

I flinched at her perkiness and asked myself

a question I'd asked a thousand times. How had I, dark and dreary, become best friends with her, sunlight and rainbows? Oh, yeah. Fifth-grade Girl Scouts. I'd misheard my mom and thought she'd enrolled me in *ghoul* scouts. To my utter disappointment it had been all badges and trefoils, not bats and zombies. Fortunately, when I burst into tears someone came to my rescue with a tissue and a Thin Mint — Coral. Despite being polar opposites, she and I had been inseparable ever since. We were like frickin' Eeyore and Tigger.

Until now. She was bouncing away for the summer.

"'Tis true I'm going to soccer camp, but I'm making it my goal to experience new things. Like in *Sisterhood of the Traveling Pants*."

I gasped. "You're going to lose your virginity to your soccer coach?"

"No! Well, maybe." She grinned and waggled her eyebrows. "Depends how hot he is."

"Coral!" I shrieked in outrage. "What's gotten into you?"

"Nothing. Yet."

I groaned and covered my ears.

She yanked my hands down. "Okay, all kidding aside. This isn't about 'losing it' before college. But when I come back from camp I want to be a new person. I'm making it my goal to get a little wilder. Get a little wiser."

"'Get down tonight,'" I sang.

Coral threw her copy of *Glamour* magazine at me. "I'm serious here," she hissed.

I held up my hands in surrender, laughing. "Okay, I get it. You're serious. You're coming back more . . . experienced."

"Exactly. Not necessarily sexually, but definitely more mature. I don't intend to have that wide-eyed, greenhorn, college freshman"— she smacked her forefinger and thumb into an L on her forehead—"loser look on my face when we get to UM."

"Hey!" I pinched her knee. "I resemble that remark."

"Chances are we both will, no matter what we do this summer, but that's not the point," she insisted.

I took a sip of my drink. "And the point is?"

"Discovery," she said, as if the answer was obvious. "Growth. Finding out just who we are."

I smirked. "You sound like a coming-of-age novel."

Her eyes widened. "That's right. That's what this is. Our coming-of-age novel, and like the song says, 'Today is where your book begins. The rest is still unwritten.'"

I shook my head, amused by her *tabula rasa* attitude. "I think mine would read more like a horror story."

"Well, there's always blood, sex, and rock and roll in those, so it couldn't be all bad," she said jokingly. "Seriously, you can change things, whatever those things are, but you need to start by getting out more this summer. By living!"

"Come on," I grumbled. "I'm here, aren't I?" I waved my hand around the glorious beach surrounding us. "It's not like I'm agoraphobic."

"No," she agreed, "but you don't date. You don't go to parties, unless I drag your ass along and then I usually have to resort to blackmail or bribery and if I'm real honest—"

"Like you'd be anything else!"

9

"You really, really need to lighten up."

"*Hmph,*" I sniffed. "I take offense at that. Did I not just laugh my butt off at Mr. Wereback?"

"Yeah, but there's lots of times where you act all emo"—she mocked one of my contemplative, semi-dejected looks—"and it wouldn't hurt you to wear some bright colors on occasion."

"Hullo!" I pointed to my bikini. "Red is bright."

"So is blue," she argued. "I'd love to see you in a baby blue that matches your eyes. With your black hair you'd look gorgy. I'm not saying you can't keep your Goth-rock style. It's you, and I love it. But you could dress it up sometimes."

I heaved a sigh. Was she right? Was I too stark? "Blue?" I asked uncertainly.

"Blue," she said emphatically.

"'Kay," I agreed. It seemed a small enough thing to do. "I can try that."

"Yes!" She beamed like I'd just offered her a winning Lotto ticket. "Since you're so agreeable, I have another homework assignment for you while I'm gone."

I shook my head. "Oh, no. You can't be

serious. It's summer. I don't do homework. Plus I just conceded a point to you."

"You can do this, too. You are required—"

"By what law?" I sassed.

"By the law vested in me"—she thumped herself on the chest—"your best friend. As I was saying, before I was so rudely interrupted, you are required to spread your wings and soar while I'm gone." She lifted her arms and flapped them slowly like large wings.

I cocked my thumb and forefinger, aimed at her, and pretended to pull the trigger. "And how am I supposed to do that when you aren't here to pitch me over the cliff?"

She leaped out of her chair. "Jump!"

I snorted. "You make it sound so easy."

"It is." She sat on the edge of my chair. "You just have to put your mind to it. Buy a new—blue—dress. Go to a party. I know Mariah's annual birthday bash is next month. And here's the biggest requirement for an A. Go on a date."

"Right," I scoffed. "No one asked me out in high school. Why would they now?"

"Who says they have to ask you?"

When I opened my mouth to object she spoke fast to stop me.

"You're the master of your destiny, Trin. Create your own path. You can do it. You can—"

"All right, all right, Confucius."

"Is that a yes?" she asked excitedly.

"Yes," I said. Anything to shut her up.

"Yes, what?" she insisted.

Drat. So much for being vague. "Yes, I'll make an effort to 'spread my wings.'"

"And?"

"And"—I clenched my teeth—"I'll buy a frickin' blue dress."

"And?"

"Corrr-al," I warned.

"And?" she persisted.

"And I'll get out more."

"On a . . ." she led.

"On a date," I barked. "Happy now?"

"Not until you pinkie promise. And no crossies."

My jaw dropped. "We haven't done that since grade school!"

"Still," she said earnestly. "This is too

important. I need to know you'll do what you say. I know you'd never break a pinkie promise."

Shit! There was no backing out now.

I clenched my fist for a moment and then popped out my pinkie. Coral wrapped hers around mine and we went through an intricate pattern of hand motions ending in a double fist bump.

Satisfied, Coral flopped back into her chair with a sigh. "Now I won't worry about you while I'm gone."

"Great," I muttered.

"And, just so you know, I'll be checking in."

"*Ter*-rific."

"Oh, come on." She gave my shoulder a playful shove. "Don't be mad, I just worry about you."

"I know," I said. How could I be mad at her for that?

"Trinity," she said, her voice dipping low and soft. "I know things haven't been easy. Especially in the last year." She studied me closely before blurting, "Your mom told me about this morning's article."

13

I closed my eyes.

And there it was.

The real reason for this trip and my summer "homework."

"So Mom put you up to this *beach day*?"

"Not exactly," Coral hedged.

I gave her a doubtful glare.

"Well, I called and said I wanted to do something today. She mentioned the article and suggested I drive us up here. She knows how much you love the beach."

I nodded. Again, I couldn't be surprised or angry.

"The bastard should've gone to jail," she said quietly.

"Yeah," I said wearily. "He should have."

"But it's not your fault, Trin. It's just not."

Wasn't it?